Praise for *Stay Up with Me*

"An intimate, acute collection—like they used to make 'em."

—*New York* magazine

"A collection of stories so astute and controlled, they stake Barbash's claim as a master of the form." —The Rumpus

"Sometimes it's hard to pinpoint the thread that binds stories in a collection together, but in the case of *Stay Up with Me*, it's enough to say that each story is very, very good. . . . Reading this book cover to cover is akin to following strangers home and staying with them just long enough to glimpse their most devastating secrets. A–." —*Entertainment Weekly*

"A truly enjoyable and funny collection of short stories, each one emotional and very well-crafted." —*InStyle* magazine

"Outstanding." —Book Riot

"The characters that populate Barbash's stories are all hurting— some of them quite badly. But it doesn't diminish their capacity for wonder." —*Mother Jones* magazine

"Winner of the Annual Book Award for The Short Story Collection Whose Characters Stuck With Me for Weeks and Months." —*Chicago Tribune*'s Biblioracle

"There's something addictive about these stories. . . . Barbash is a true craftsman who sweats over every sentence, and the artistry makes you want to read the next story. [His] stories remind me of a really good A.A. meeting, one where the old-timers aren't showing off but the people who are genuinely in pain are tearing their hearts out. . . . Such people need to talk, they need to cry, they need to feel sorry for themselves and Barbash lets them. That takes a lot of courage for a person, and a lot of courage for a writer." —Clancy Martin, *New York Times Book Review*

"Tom Barbash's *Stay Up with Me* surprised me in a big way. I fell immediately into it and did the zombie walk, with it open, to the couch. Where I stayed until I'd read half the book and parental obligations intruded. I don't do that all that often and I definitely don't do that with short-story collections. . . . *Stay Up with Me* is exactly the book I'd want on a train or airplane trip, the kind that makes me look up at fellow travelers and imagine them having lives like the ones on these pages."
    —Mary Pols, MSN's Page Turner Top Shelf Pick

"A piercing first collection that explores characters reacting to the chaos and consequences of their everyday lives, from fractured relationships to the loss of a loved one and instant regret. Barbash's thirteen sharply eloquent tales are intricately shaded by his characters' desires." —*Booklist*

"What makes this new collection so distinctive is Barbash's successful appropriation of the Upper West Side as his own literary realm. No other writer has written about that part of the world the way he does." —Antonio Ruiz-Camacho, Kirkus' Features

"Barbash's stories are remarkable for their dark humor, elegant renderings of awkward family dynamics, and emotional intensity."

—PW Daily

"You may recognize a piece of yourself in each character featured in this eminently readable collection."

—*American Way* magazine

"Barbash strips things down to their essentials, and the effect is to bring the reader in as close as possible. Often it seems as if these are stories being whispered by a person who witnessed the actual events."

—*Aspen Times*

"Graceful. If Raymond Carver had lived in Manhattan he might have delivered stories like 'The Break' . . . or 'Balloon Night.'"

—*Kirkus Reviews*

"Barbash is a strong storyteller who has mastered the architecture of the short story, right down to the tender, subdued prose that delights in sharp details."

—*Publishers Weekly*

"This appealing collection reveals a supple writer who draws us in from the start of each new story, with none of the 'collection fatigue' one sometimes feels along the way from even the best practitioners of the genre. Highly recommended."

—*Library Journal*

Stay Up
with Me

STORIES

TOM BARBASH

ecco

An Imprint of HarperCollins*Publishers*

STAY UP WITH ME. Copyright © 2013 by Tom Barbash. All rights reserved. Printed in the United States of America. No part of this book may be used or reproduced in any manner whatsoever without written permission except in the case of brief quotations embodied in critical articles and reviews. For information address HarperCollins Publishers, 10 East 53rd Street, New York, NY 10022.

HarperCollins books may be purchased for educational, business, or sales promotional use. For information please e-mail the Special Markets Department at SPsales@harpercollins.com.

A hardcover edition of this book was published in 2013 by Ecco, an imprint of HarperCollins Publishers.

FIRST ECCO PAPERBACK EDITION PUBLISHED 2014.

Library of Congress Cataloging-in-Publication Data has been applied for.

ISBN 978-0-06-225813-7

14 15 16 17 18   OV/RRD   10 9 8 7 6 5 4 3 2 1

For James

Grateful acknowledgment is made to the publications in which the following stories first appeared: "The Break" in *Tin House* and *Distinguished Story—Best American Stories;* "Balloon Night" in *One Story* and on *Selected Shorts;* "Her Words" in *StoryQuarterly;* "Howling at the Moon" in *Chicago Tribune* (Nelson Algren Award Winner); "Somebody's Son" in *Press;* "How to Fall" in *Zyzzyva;* "Letters from the Academy" in *McSweeney's;* "January" in *Greensboro Review;* "Stay Up with Me" in *Missouri Review;* "Paris" in *South Carolina Review;* "Spectator" in *Virginia Quarterly Review;* "Birthday Girl" in *McSweeney's;* "The Women" in *Narrative, Best American Non-Required Reading.*

THE BREAK

It was her son's second night home for Christmas break, and the mother had taken him to a pizza place on Columbus Avenue called Buongiorno, their favorite. The boy was enjoying all the attention. The conversation revolved around him and his friends. He was talking about someone in school who had lost her mind, a pale, pretty girl who'd been institutionalized and who sent a scrawled-over copy of *The Great Gatsby* to a friend of the boy's. In the margins, she had pointed out all the similarities between the character's situation and what she believed to be hers and that of the boy's friend. She had earmarked pages and scrawled messages. YOU ARE GATSBY, she wrote on the back of the book. I AM DAISY.

The boy's mother pictured the girl in a hospital ward, aligning her fortunes with tragic heroines, ripping through the classics with a pen. At least, the boy's mother thought, the insanity was literary. They were taking school seriously, she thought, and she liked that her son seemed to have some compassion for the woman (more than she did; she was simply glad it wasn't he who'd been the target).

She liked the person he was becoming, liked the way he treated others. He'd had a girlfriend in the spring and then another over the summer and the mother had liked how he opened doors for them, how he listened to what they said, and how he talked of them when they weren't around. Now both of those were over and done with. She didn't know much about how they'd ended, only that he'd kept in touch with one and not the other. From time to time the boy glanced toward the front door of the restaurant at the hostess station. The hostess smiled over at them. The boy's mother was getting used to this. Her son had begun to fill out in the last year, his sophomore year at college, and had become the sort of young man women smiled at, and not only girls his age. Recently one of the mother's friends saw a picture of him in a T-shirt and jeans and had said, "*Look out.*"

The pizza was good and the boy ate a lot of it. The mother looked over and caught the eye of the hostess. A good ten years older than the boy, and not what you'd call pretty. Though thin and busty, she had a somewhat pinched nose and a dull cast to her eyes. The mother imagined that she often went home with men she met at the restaurant. The girls the son had dated were smart and pretty and charming. This woman was not. Her son didn't seem to notice her but was talking about the coming summer and how he wanted to travel around Eastern Europe, Romania maybe, or Hungary. He'd work half the summer and then take off. He wasn't going to ask for any money, he said. "How's the book going?" he asked the mother.

She had been writing a book about Hollywood in the 1950s. She told him about the last three chapters, one on the advent of television and the other two on the end of the studio system. He asked good questions, made suggestions. He was funny. He was her friend.

He left for a moment for the bathroom. The mother watched the hostess watching her son as he crossed the room, as though he were a chef's special she was hoping to try. The hostess walked back toward the kitchen. The mother couldn't see either of them now. *It's nothing,* she told herself.

But then she was peering around the partition to see what was happening. The hostess was lingering eight or ten feet from the men's room. *How incredibly pathetic,* the mother thought.

The boy stepped out. She said something. He said something. Then he was back at the table.

"Should we get dessert?"

"What did that woman say to you?"

"Nothing."

"I saw her say *something.*"

"Oh, you know, How's it going? How's your meal?"

She was acting like a jealous wife, she thought.

"I think she likes you," the mother said, though not encouragingly.

The boy smiled, then changed the subject.

They stopped at an ice-cream place on the way home, a store the boy had worked at three summers before. Back home they watched the second half of *Anatomy of a Murder* on TV, then the mother said she was going to sleep. The boy stayed in the family room to watch more TV.

The mother read for a while. She thought of calling her husband, but then didn't because she would probably bring up the hostess, then feel ridiculous for doing so. She'd make it a bigger deal than it needed to be. It had been a nice night, she thought. They'd have a few weeks of these and then he'd be gone again, and she'd be alone in the house. She liked his company, and lately she'd been starting to understand that *this* was the reward for all the work you did, these years of friendship. You watched them become the sort of people you wanted to know.

In the middle of the night she heard voices and she wondered if he'd turned the volume up too loud. She walked back to the family room. The doors were partially open. She peered in and there was the hostess, her shirt off and one of her considerable breasts in her son's mouth. Her son's shirt was off, and his eyes were closed. The hostess was straddling the boy's lap, her chin resting atop his head as he nursed and nuzzled.

She stepped back out and closed the door.

"Shit," she heard the boy say.

The mother was surprised by what she felt then—not embarrassed, even for him. She felt enraged and invaded, as though someone had broken into her home and stolen something valuable.

"Can you come out here a moment?" the mother said.

He walked out, his hair messed, but his pants still on.

"I'd like her to leave."

His eyes were on the ground. He looked ashamed, and she knew she wasn't being entirely fair here.

"And keep your voices down."

She tried to pinpoint what it was exactly that bothered her about the hostess because she wouldn't have minded if it were her son's girlfriend over. She was neither a prude nor a moralist.

There was something about her son picking up a stranger

and bringing her back, and using a dinner out with her to do it, that made her feel used and betrayed.

Then she thought: *He's nineteen. He can do what he likes.*

She heard the two of them leave through the front door. Her son was walking the woman home, she supposed, which was the right thing to do.

Around twenty minutes later he'd returned. He didn't knock on her door to complain or apologize. He went to his room and closed the door.

They said nothing about the incident at breakfast the next morning. They read different sections of the paper and talked about what classes he was taking in spring.

The next day the mother was walking to the subway and she passed the pizza place. The hostess looked up from her seating list and saw her through the window. They made eye contact. The hostess smiled, affably and unappealingly (one of her teeth might have been gray). The mother kept walking.

The mother made dinner that night, rosemary chicken and steamed vegetables. The boy was going out with some friends afterward. The mother knew the friends, Oscar, whose father was a producer for *Nightline,* and Kevin, a math major at Dartmouth who always smelled of coffee. The boy was not home by two o'clock, nor by three. At around four he returned. She thought better of confronting him. There were things she wouldn't know, and that would have to be okay. Still, she dreamed that night that he'd brought home two women, strippers, and they had tied him to the leather armchair in the family room.

* * *

She said nothing the next day. Her work was going slowly. She tried to keep her mind on Howard Hawks and Elia Kazan, but her thoughts kept returning to the hostess. She had altered the atmosphere surrounding the boy's time home. And now the mother was having trouble meeting her self-imposed deadlines. She went by the restaurant the following afternoon after the lunch tables had cleared. The hostess was refilling hot pepper and grated cheese dispensers.

"Do you know who I am?" the mother asked, when she stopped by.

"You're Phillip's mother."

She didn't like her using his name, though of course it would have been strange for her not to know it by now. "Yes," she said.

"I'm Holly." She said it as though the mother had heard all about someone named Holly.

"He's nineteen, you know."

"I know."

"It's none of my business."

"No, I guess it isn't. Can I get you a table?"

She talked with her husband that day. She didn't tell him what she'd seen, simply that Phillip was dating a hostess from Buongiorno's.

"So?"

"So I don't like it."

"Don't be such a snob."

"You haven't seen her."

"What's wrong with her?"

"You'd know if you saw her," she said. Then added, "She's easy."

"How do you know?"

"I saw the two of them."

"You saw them."

"You know."

"Having sex."

"Practically."

"Do you want me to talk with him?"

"No. I just wanted to know what you think."

"I think it's fairly normal, don't you?"

It was nearly two years since the mother and father had decided to undergo a trial separation. The mother had believed it was her decision, because he had fought it. But once they'd gone through with it, he had more easily adapted to the new set of circumstances. Now the husband lived in Seattle, a few blocks from the fish and vegetable stalls of Pike Place Market. The mother had spent time there in graduate school, and then again two years ago when they'd decided to travel around the Pacific Northwest. She hadn't known then he'd been thinking of moving there, once the boy left for college. He was the one who was supposed to be exiled, but while he had landed within a lively social circle, the mother had found it hard to find any sort of community. She had been the less social of the two and now she was in his town with his friends. There were three or four people who stuck closely by her, but most of their friends had stopped calling or inviting her to parties. Not that she would have gone, necessarily. She hadn't been feeling particularly social. She was abstractly aware of the toll the separation had taken on her. She'd been needing a glass of red wine or two in the evening to get to sleep, and some nights she couldn't resist calling him, knowing it was the West Coast and he'd still be awake. She wouldn't talk about their problems, she'd simply talk of her day and matters outside of them and then listen to his advice, or she'd ask about his life out there and he'd tell her, as though they were new friends beginning to learn about one another. Her work meanwhile had flourished; she'd finished one book, started another, and had begun contributing magazine pieces. There were many times when she thought to herself, *I love my life*, but they were all times when she was alone and wrapped inside her writing, or reading, or out on a long sumptuous walk in Central Park. She had grown to respect and learn from solitude, something she'd had little of in the past. Another good thing was that she'd become closer to her son. In the past she'd felt like a supporting actress to her husband's incessant starring role. Now when the boy came home it was easy, like having a great roommate. He cooked sometimes, or at least set the table and did the dishes. They talked about everything, except the boy's father. She knew they were still close, but the boy seemed to understand the competition between his parents. He'd made the mother feel as though he was on her side without ever really taking sides. She pictured her husband's life out there amid Starbucks and Microsoft. He was working now for a software company in new product development. He had stock shares. He had a kayak and a mountain bike. He was fifty, and he still looked thirty-five. She was forty-five and looked it. She imagined her husband with a younger woman. And when she pressed the boy after his visit west for Thanksgiving, he affirmed there was someone younger who the father was occasionally seeing. Someone thirty.

Friday night they went out to a movie together, a black comedy her son had been talking about for days, and afterward they

walked the fifteen blocks home. The boy had laughed through-
out, but now she was dissecting the story, explaining how it could
have been better. She was pointing out inconsistencies in the
plot, and funny parts she'd found more depressing than funny,
until she saw that she was essentially ruining his experience of it.

"I guess it did kind of suck," he said.

"Don't you ever just go to a movie to enjoy it?" her husband
asked, when he called that night. This had been a favorite argument of theirs.

"Sure," she said. "But I don't enjoy crap. I wish I did. I'm
tired of disliking things."

As she went to sleep that night she heard her son slipping out.
Without thinking of what she was doing, she threw on her long
coat and boots and followed him, her nightgown underneath. The
night was cold and mostly empty. A homeless man slept at the
door of a dry cleaner's. A few bankers or lawyers scuttled home
for a few hours' sleep; others, ties loosened, were out having late
drinks around window tables of the neighborhood eateries. Most
of the stores were decorated for Christmas with lights and Santas;
the Gap had a reindeer in a down vest. A thin man with small
wire-rimmed glasses waited while his dog watered a bare tree.
The boy walked by the restaurant and picked up the hostess.
When she walked out the door, they rounded a corner and kissed
hungrily, illicitly, like adulterers in a bad movie when they've
sneaked from the dinner party into the kitchen. Having seen him
in love before, and sweetly, it was odd and depressing to see him
this way: as a man with an impersonal libido.

He talked animatedly to her as they walked. *About what?* the mother wondered, and then she realized he was describing a scene from the movie they'd been to. He stopped in the middle of the block to finish, the streetlight above him casting his gestures in long, graceful shadows. The action sounded so much more compelling in his words than it had been on the screen; he had in fact added details and lines of dialogue that improved it. He was similar to his father in that way. Anything that happened sounded better coming from her son. It occurred to the mother that he was better suited for enjoying the world than she was. The boy laughed and the hostess just watched him. She kissed him seductively, her hands running from his chest to his shoulders. And then she did something that made the mother queasy. She ran her hand between his legs. It happened so fast the mother wasn't sure she hadn't rubbed his thigh or grasped for something in his front pocket.

"*Helloo,*" the hostess said.

He's a college sophomore, the mother wanted to say. He still plays knock-hockey with his friends who come over, still collects rare stamps.

They went and had a drink at a nearby tavern. The mother watched through a window as the boy ordered drinks at the bar and brought them back to the table. It had gotten colder out, the wind had hardened, and the mother thought briefly of returning home. She was driven by curiosity, or perhaps by the impulse that causes some people to watch cars crash into each other, or fires overtake homes. At the same time she felt protective of the son she'd raised. She supposed fathers went through this all the time with their daughters—the sudden and alarming realization that their offspring had become eye candy for the masses, not simply for the right boys, who would be scrutinized and carefully selected. The hostess leaned ahead, resting her assets on the table before her. She was making girlish facial expressions, attempting to present herself as his age, which she definitely wasn't. She wasn't old. She was between their ages. The same age, the mother thought, as the woman who dated the boy's father. She imagined the two of them in Seattle after the boy graduated, double-dating roommates, sisters perhaps, who would argue when they were together in the women's room who would get Dad and who'd sleep with Junior.

At the moment she'd decided to head home, she heard her name called. She turned and started walking, but the voice followed. "Elaine. Elaine, is that you?"

She stopped then; it was Joyce Taft, from the fifth floor of her apartment building.

"Hi, Joyce."

"I thought so. Are you all right? I saw you standing out here. It's awfully cold out."

"Yes, I'm fine."

Joyce was examining her, as if hunting for clues to explain this behavior. The mother wondered if the neck of her nightgown was showing above her coat. She thought she should say something else so she said, "I just came out to clear my head."

Joyce nodded and the mother understood she would soon become a story Joyce would tell to a half-dozen people in the building: *She's been like that ever since Warren moved out.*

"I'm heading home, if you'd like company," Joyce said.

The mother looked at the window; they were walking toward the front cash register.

"Thanks, sure," the mother said.

* * *

He was back home at around five. The mother and the boy didn't see each other until the early evening.

That night as they stood in the kitchen, she managed to get him to say he'd been seeing the hostess.

"I don't want you to see her again," she said.

"Why not?"

"Because I don't."

"I like her."

"You like her."

"I do," he said, as though defending a great principle.

"Is she your girlfriend?"

"No."

"What is she?"

"She's a friend. Am I getting the fifth degree here? Do I need a lawyer present?"

"You can do what you want."

"I've had a good week."

She didn't know what he meant by the comment.

"Go ahead and screw her if you want," she said, unfortunately, pointlessly.

Her boy did a strange thing then. He started crying.

He didn't go out that night or the next. He watched TV on his own, or read in her study. He wasn't friendly or particularly unfriendly.

After three nights of this, the mother asked, "What happened to the hostess?"

"Nothing," he said.

"Nothing?"

"I blew her off."

And that was that. He went out with friends that weekend and for a few nights did nothing. She'd walk by the hostess and draw looks and then she stopped walking by.

One day on her way home she felt the hostess following her.

"What did you tell him?" the hostess said.

The mother turned and faced her. The hostess had on a thick navy turtleneck sweater over tight black jeans. She had a small stack of Buongiorno's menus in one hand, as though to remind the mother of where she'd just sprung from.

"I told him I didn't want him seeing you."

"Why?"

"Because I don't want him to. He's nineteen, what are you?"

"Twenty-eight."

"He's just a kid."

"No he's not." She raised her eyebrows. "*Believe* me, he's not."

The mother's hand jumped out and slapped the woman. The woman slapped the mother back, and then they were yelling at each other and swinging their arms. A waiter and the stout old manager ran out to break it up.

"Pathetic bitch," the hostess said beneath her breath.

She had always imagined a life for her son that would exceed her own: more travel, better clothes and food, a little land maybe, near a body of water; an unimpeachably bright, elegant, and decent partner, whom the mother could imagine as a daughter, the one she'd never had, for whom she could now buy sweaters and stylish scarves and sign the gift cards *Love, Elaine.* But what if what she wanted wasn't what he wanted? What if this hostess was what he wanted? Her awful little apartment, her abject little life. And what if they had children and they looked not like him at all but like her? She pictured two children, four and six with the hostess's face, those small dull eyes and those sunken nostrils.

It occurred to her the hostess would tell her son about the incident. She'd describe the mother as crazy, and the boy might agree.

She called the boy's father and there was no answer. It was eleven thirty New York time. She tried again at one and reached him. After a little banter about her writing, he asked, "What's up?"

"I hit her," she said, surprised at her own disclosure. "And she hit me back."

"Who?"

"The hostess."

The line went silent, and the mother considered telling him she was joking.

"You hit her?"

"Yes. It was a mistake, okay? But she hit me as well. The people from the restaurant broke it up."

"I don't know what to say. Let it go. It's his life. Jesus, Elaine, you hit her?"

"I didn't call to be *upbraided*."

She dreamed that night the hostess was pregnant and that she'd given her son a disease.

* * *

She didn't see the hostess in the restaurant window after that. One day she saw in the doorway the manager who'd broken up the fight. She asked him what had happened to the hostess.

"We let her go," he said.

"Over the incident?" the mother asked.

"Yes, of course. We don't condone that kind of thing. I hope you and your husband will come back and eat with us again," the man said.

Two days later she met with her editor. They went to lunch to talk about the new pages, which were about the failed-birthday-party scene in *East of Eden* (the moment that launched the late 1950s and '60s youth culture, she postulated) and the influence of the Beats and the French new wave, and when the mother returned to the office, she found herself speaking at great length on all these subjects with the receptionist, a sophomore at Bowdoin College in Maine, an English major, with green eyes and lovely teeth, who wanted someday to be an editor. She had read the mother's last two books.

"What I loved about them both was how personal they were. Whatever you're writing about it's as if you're speaking to one person, to a good friend. That's what you make the reader feel like. You made me feel like it. I felt smart reading your books; smarter than I usually feel, anyhow." She laughed.

There were still ten days left in her son's vacation.

"Do you have a boyfriend?" the mother asked.

They would go to the movies and then get Indian food. He was doing her a favor, the mother said, because the girl might end up editing one of her books someday. The night started slowly, but before long the boy was telling his stories, and the girl listening, then telling a few of her own. The mother prodded them both with questions. They had much in common, she thought. But there were enough differences for them to learn from one another. When the girl excused herself to go to the restroom, the mother said, "Is this awkward? I mean my coming along like this."

The boy smiled, "No. It's kind of fun really. It's like being on the *Charlie Rose* show."

"I'll head home after this and you can do whatever you want."

On their walk back to the apartment the girl asked more questions of the mother, how and where she worked, which authors she liked to read. Many of them the girl too had read. What was gratifying was how well the boy held his own in the conversation. He was never entirely an intellectual, but he was smart, and inquisitive, and there was reason to believe he'd grow into an interesting, expansive adult, given the right company. Already they were laughing easily at each other's jokes. And besides, there was nothing wrong with the fact that the girl was a knockout, at least by the mother's standards.

Christmas Eve the mother filled the boy's old red-and-white stocking with candy he wouldn't eat, a book, and two CDs she knew he wanted. The next morning they listened to Christmas carols and opened their gifts. She encouraged the boy to open his father's gifts in front of her. There was a beautiful blue ski parka, to accompany the skis she had bought him (they'd worked this out weeks ago on the phone) and, as a surprise to the mother and the boy, a laptop computer.

She had been outspent again, but she didn't mind.

She had given him something better.

They saw each other the next three evenings, and they were planning on going to a New Year's Eve party at a SoHo restaurant that the girl's high school friends had rented out. The mother got them theater tickets for a show on December 29, and this time she resisted going with them. She would go to a late movie by herself so that they could get settled in the apartment after the show. Part of this, she knew, was an attempt to make up for getting in his way with the hostess, but he'd someday understand, or maybe he already did.

It had turned out so well, she thought. He seemed happier. The girl could visit him at school. And the mother thought there were advantages to having a girlfriend at another college. First of all, long-distance relationships were often the most romantic. Second of all, they left you more time for your friends and your schoolwork. Relationships in college were difficult to maintain. There were so many distractions, and those distractions were healthy. The boy was on an intramural basketball team and played bass guitar in a band. It didn't matter that by his own admission the team wasn't very good and neither was the band. She didn't want him to have to give up anything.

The night they went to the theater, the mother went to a late showing of a trite Tom Hanks movie that was set in her neighborhood and made it look like a decent place to fall in love. When she returned, she was pleased to hear the sound of the stereo, of the two of them staying up late. She peered in before she went to sleep at midnight, and they were together on the couch looking at an atlas. The boy was showing her where he planned to travel over the summer. The mother pictured them in a curtained train compartment, rolling through the Romanian countryside, poring over a guidebook.

"Good night, you two," she said.

And her son blew her a kiss.

When she woke again, it was two thirty or maybe three and the music was playing still, or again. She went to get herself a glass of water. They were talking, and though she still felt hazy and half asleep, she realized it wasn't the girl's voice she was hearing. The girl was gone, and somehow he'd managed to get the hostess to come over for a nightcap. Tag team. *Here come the reinforcements.* It gave her a terrible sinking feeling. She retreated into her room and tried to remind herself that it was his life and that he was over eighteen and could do what he wanted. But the more time passed and the more she thought of the two of them in there, the angrier she got. Not merely on her own behalf, but on behalf of the girl. It was so ugly and pointless what the boy was doing, so soulless. She tried to go to sleep again and forget it all but she couldn't help placing herself in the girl's shoes. She might be thinking of the boy right now, and of the countries they'd visit together. And tomorrow when they went out again, the boy would tell her nothing of what he'd done with the hostess, nor would he seem different.

She wouldn't abide this. Not in her house, and not with a woman she'd come to blows with, no matter whose fault it had been. She walked to the study and threw the doors open.

"I want you to get *the fuck* out of here," she said.

But there was no one in the room except the boy. He was

alone watching TV. There was a bowl of ice cream before him and a can of 7UP.

He seemed not angry then but frightened, the way one might feel while watching a spouse put her hand through a glass door panel, which her husband had watched her do. It happened in the period when she'd thought he'd been screwing around. He hadn't, though he admitted he'd come close once. The boy never knew anything of this.

Now he was walking toward the mother. She was crying soundlessly, and she felt as though she might never stop.

"My God, Mom, what's going on? What's this about?"

On the TV the woman, Barbara Stanwyck, was running her fingers through Henry Fonda's hair. The mother had seen the movie a half-dozen times, but she'd managed not to recognize the dialogue.

"I thought . . ."

"I know . . . I know," he said. He said it as one might say it to a child who'd thought she heard a ghost.

She didn't have to explain anything, she realized; he knew her better than she did right then and maybe he had for a while. Her son. It was as though her irrational behavior had promoted him to the role of the wise and clement adult. And while she felt significant pride in this, she feared now that he'd plan to spend his coming vacations in Seattle, or Europe, or Colorado. He was unlikely to spend another Christmas in New York with her.

"Come on," he said, as though reading her thoughts. "Let's watch the rest of this."

"All right," she said, and she let him fill her in on what she'd missed.

Before the end of the movie, he fell asleep. She turned the TV off and threw a blanket over him.

It was four now, one o'clock in Seattle. There was an off chance he could still be up, but of course there was no guarantee he would be alone. She imagined calling him, and him consoling her with his new girlfriend in bed next to him, and afterward, he'd say, "She's still having a rough time of it." And it would even score points with the woman who would see how gracious and tolerant he was. She thought then about the hostess, because it was she who had started all this. What was it the mother had hated so much? She was no criminal, and she hadn't treated the boy badly as far as the mother knew.

She had simply seemed too desperate, too lonely, too hungry. Her needs were too naked. The mother could imagine someone like that consuming her boy, swallowing him up, before he had the chance to see the world and become the person she knew he could be. He snored softly now, with the beginnings of a cold, she knew, because when he was a child it would begin that way: a mild sawing sound, a sniffle the next morning, and a temperature the following night. She would douse it with soups and juices, and she would secretly enjoy the days he was too sick to go to school and had to stay home with her. It was in the time they'd first moved to the Village, in that odd little apartment on Tenth Street with the stained-glass window and the false fireplace they bottom-lit to resemble embers, and the acres of built-in bookshelves, and the café down the street where they'd listen to bad poetry, and the tiny crowded market where she'd buy bread and fish. Her husband would be reading in bed, waiting for her. She would watch her sleeping son for ten minutes or twenty, and marvel at all his possibilities, a life that young, so full of wonder and unstained hope.

BALLOON NIGHT

imkin's wife left him during a blisteringly cold Thanksgiving week, two nights before their annual Balloon Night party. There was no time for Timkin to call their guests and cancel; nor would he know where to call in many cases. It was the sort of event attended by people from all corners of their lives whether or not they could produce a fresh invite. Once invited always invited, he and Amy had said.

The Timkins had a three-bedroom eighth-floor apartment, on West Seventy-Seventh Street between Central Park West and Columbus, the balloon block. It was where those cloud-size cartoon characters for the Macy's Thanksgiving Day Parade were inflated, the night before Thanksgiving, and nearly all the residents would open their apartment doors to anyone and everyone they knew. Timkin grew up in the apartment (which his parents had ceded to him six years earlier when they moved to Naples, Florida) and had attended his first balloon party at age six. Now he was thirty-four.

Timkin had been too depressed to tell anyone the dismal news, and in truth he had convinced himself that Amy would return, apologetic, or demanding an apology, which he would provide, and they would make up at dinner and in bed that night, and it would all blow over. He couldn't even remember what they'd fought about, only that it was insignificant and he had been right.

The first two days after Amy had walked out Timkin rode his bike around the island of Manhattan in a fog, dodging trucks and taxis, heading down to Battery Park, through Chinatown and the Village, and then up Sixth Avenue. He was at least in part on the lookout for Amy, but he did not go by the building where she worked. On day three he went in to his office and tried to keep busy, but mostly just stared at the phone, and composed on his computer the germs of letters to Amy, alternating fragments of forgiveness and bitterness.

The guests would begin arriving at nine, and so at six Timkin went by himself to the Pioneer grocery on Columbus to get Coke and Sprite and scotch and beer and wine, then over to Citarella for assorted cheeses and pâtés, a few flat bread pizzas, caviar, salmon, the oilier dill-covered kind they called *Grav Lox,* dips, crackers, bread and carpaccio, and pumpkin and pecan pie. Spent a fortune. But he could pull this off. He would make the best of a terrible situation, and he could tell them *something,* that he'd get through this, though he wasn't convinced he would. The balloons and the alcohol might be a distraction, no? Could you stay depressed with a decent scotch in your paper cup, and Underdog smiling overhead?

You could of course. And then he wondered: Did he have to tell them?

Eventually he'd need to, if the break were real. But telling everyone now was a bit like telling people you were pregnant one week after reading the home pregnancy test. So many things could change. And anyhow, would it harm anything, for the purposes of the party, to say his wife was away for a few days on business? Amy worked in advertising, on the account side, and was quite often away.

But away for Thanksgiving?

She'd be back on Thursday evening at around 6:30, Timkin decided, and they'd have dinner with Amy's parents on the East Side. She was heartbroken that she couldn't be there, he'd tell his guests, and they would all drink a toast to her.

It could work, Timkin thought. He pictured Amy arriving at Kennedy in her red wool jacket and then cabbing back to East Eighty-Fourth Street, and then he suddenly felt a warm surge of relief settle over him, which was very much like having her back. He could postpone his suffering for a night, why the heck not? He suddenly felt good, better than he had in weeks. And he went back to his bathroom to shave and dress, and put on his best game face.

First arriving were the Willises, a sportswriter for the *New York Times* and his wife, Sabrina, who owned a small absurdly expensive beauty salon in the East Twenties. They'd been better friends with Amy, so there was the risk they'd know. But the leaving had only just happened on Monday, and besides, Timkin and Amy had been notoriously out of touch with their friends lately, perhaps as a result of their feuding, or because their jobs had been so exhausting.

Jonah Willis covered college football, which meant he traveled a lot on weekends.

"The bad news is that Amy can't be here tonight. She's

heartbroken," Timkin said. "She's staying in a little Marriott in Cincinnati of all places."

"Oh God," Sabrina said. "They're really cutting back. I bet I know what she's doing there. She's making a P&G stop, isn't she?"

"You might know her better than I do," Timkin said, smiling and fearing it might be true.

The apartment was immaculate. Timkin, after all, was the clean one of the two. Amy's untidiness had been an issue, but not a particularly significant one. Timkin liked finding the occasional book left out, or magazine article; he liked seeing where Amy had left off, and when they were first dating, he often tried to guess the last sentence she'd read before she put the book down. He'd tell her sometimes which one he thought and more often than not he'd get it right.

At some point she started telling him it was a different line or a different page altogether. And then she stopped leaving her books open just to avoid the conversation.

But the place was neat now. And there were still some of her things around, though she'd taken most of her clothes. Only one or two of her old coats remained in the closet, and Timkin wondered if the closet's relative emptiness would clue anyone in to what had transpired. He could say she'd taken a few coats with her on her trip . . . but that was a bit ridiculous, wasn't it? It wasn't a crime scene after all.

In truth, Amy had been happy lately, or happier than a lot of other times in the years Timkin had known her. She was taking classes after work, dance and French, painting and Pilates. And she was more confident and self-willed, Timkin thought. He encouraged her to follow her interests. She had taken him twice to her wine tasting class and on their way home the second time he had poked fun at the comically pretentious instructor. She appeared hurt by his comments, as though he'd insulted her and not the silly wine guy. "How about *you* take the class and when we go to restaurants, you can pick the wine. I won't mind," he said.

"But I'll want you to know the difference," she said.

Once he suggested she was pretending to like movies that secretly bored her and for two days she was notably distant from him. He'd only meant to tease her. Eventually she told him—in the morning as she left for work—"I respond to things that aren't obvious, and that doesn't make me fake or a bad person. I can't change what I like to suit you."

But he did that *all the time*, he could have said. It was part of being a successful couple, he believed: the capacity to adapt.

"Can I open this one?" Willis asked. It was a bottle of eighteen-year-old Laphroaig Timkin had been saving for tonight, and he smiled.

"Dig in," he said, happy for the chance to feel generous.

He had a nice-size scotch and the warmth of it—and the prospect of seeing all his friends and Amy's friends and their families tonight—made Timkin feel loved, and he allowed himself to believe that Amy might actually return tonight, that it wasn't out of the question. She understood the spirit of this event; she'd know how much it would mean to Timkin if she suddenly turned up. Just last year a former colleague of Amy's had done exactly that. She and Amy had a falling-out before the woman left the agency, but when they saw each other at the party, all was forgiven.

They embraced for several seconds. Timkin had watched this.

It could happen just like that, he thought.

"How's work?" Willis asked, and Timkin, who taught history at City College and wrote biographies, told him his prepared answer, that he was around halfway through the book, that the research was mostly done and now he had follow-up interviews and a good chunk of writing ahead. He might try to get out of the city to do it, upstate somewhere.

"Amy's going to let you get away?"

"What's good for the goose," he said.

"I suppose," Sabrina said. "You guys must go crazy spending that much time apart."

"I don't like it," Timkin said. "It's just a fact of life."

He took another belt of scotch and then the doorbell rang. It was the Schwabackers from the fourth floor, Eric and Dana, sporty and blond. He was a lawyer and she was a postdoctoral fellow in neuroscience, something with fruit flies. Every time she explained her work to Timkin his mind drifted out the window and across the park where it sat down at a restaurant somewhere on the East Side. A lot of people's stories about their work bored him, but he always asked about it anyway—better to never ask, no?

Now came a few of his old college friends, Seth, and Jordan and Lilia and their whole crowd who tended to stay by themselves at one side of the apartment, in the kitchen usually, rarely branching out to talk with anyone else, though they'd seen these same people here every year. His aunt Eileen arrived then with his cousins, Monique and Andrew. Kisses all around and each time he had to tell them, "She couldn't get out of it, she's absolutely miserable about it."

"She couldn't get someone else to go?" Eileen asked.

"I guess it doesn't work that way. Anyhow, Amy said we shouldn't have too much fun or she'll be horribly jealous."

"The hell with that," said Lilia who'd been listening in. "Let's make her miserably and inconsolably jealous."

"How would we do that?" asked Eric.

"Use your imagination," Lilia said.

A woman Timkin didn't know was walking about taking drink orders, and then a whole group of people he'd never set eyes on before entered his apartment. This was the chaos of Balloon Night. Everyone in every building on the block that ran along the south side of the Museum of Natural History was having a party, and the guests roamed from floor to floor like fish into diverging streams. The doormen had lists, and beyond that, the cops at the corner crossing blocks had lists to determine whom they'd allow onto the block itself.

Still, with all this security, there were always twenty or so people at Timkin's party he didn't know, and often they would be the ones who stayed the longest.

"Come on in," he said graciously to four strangers, wondering who they knew. "Is Jordan here?" one of them eventually said, and Timkin pointed the way.

Timkin had downed three decent-size scotches by the time Snoopy sprouted limbs. He peered down at the street at the lot of them, Garfield, and some dinosaur he couldn't name, and Big Bird, and Kermit and two M&M's and some newer cartoon characters whose names he had yet to learn (some yellow Pokémon thing), illuminated by klieg lights in the dark night. As a child it had looked like an army of giant aliens had taken over his street.

Back inside he started to inventory the guests. There were more of his friends here than hers now, but a few high school and college chums of Amy's had entered the party without his noticing, and he would have to tell them his story about her being away.

From conversational snippets he could hear things like, "*Poor thing*. In an awful hotel at a sales conference." Or "I heard they cancelled her flight."

"I haven't talked to Amy in so long," said her friend from Middlebury College, Melanie, whom Timkin had always had a thing for. "I can't believe she'd miss this."

"She was so heartbroken over it," Timkin said, and then maybe too quickly switching the subject, "*You* look healthy and happy."

"It's what joblessness and poverty do to you."

"What happened?"

"It's too long a story. Part of that oppressive cloud that's been hanging over the New York theater world. I'm sleeping on someone's floor right now. How about you?"

"I'm good," Timkin said.

"How so?"

He tried to think of an answer.

"Because the world can still produce things like this." He gestured around the room.

"A bunch of irritatingly bourgeois people holding drinks?"

"The whole thing. I depend on it."

"It's good fun if you look at it the right way," Melanie said. "You know, I never really thought that Amy liked this."

"Oh, she does," Timkin said. "It's her favorite night of the year."

She looked at him. "If you say so."

Timkin noticed Melanie's empty drink glass. As he went to fill her order, someone slapped his back—Malcolm from his Saturday-morning basketball game.

"I love these parties. And you know *why?*" Malcolm was looking at Melanie as he pondered this. Timkin didn't wait for the answer because he saw three older couples walk into his apartment, business associates of his father's and their wives, all of whom would stay for around forty-five minutes and then leave for another party in the building. Happened every year. They brought expensive wine and spent most of their time talking to Amy, who had a way with the older set.

Malcolm was attempting to corner Melanie who managed to slip away and across the apartment. There were several people leaning their heads and torsos out of the window like kids and yelling at the cartoon characters below.

The Svenvolds were still in their coats, and so Timkin helped remove them and carried them into his bedroom, hers a fitted trench with a plaid inlay, and his, a long, gray cashmere coat that Timkin would love to own.

He liked the style of his parents' friends, their breadth of experience and flowery elegance; their love of old jazz standards and good stiff drinks. Not infrequently Timkin wished that he'd lived in their day because he didn't always feel suited to his own. Especially not now after what had happened.

"Here comes the Road Runner," someone yelled.

"That isn't the *Road Runner*," Malcolm yelled back. "There's no fucking Road Runner."

There were now well-entrenched crowds in the kitchen, the foyer, in the dining room and living room—and in all three bedrooms were smaller circles, friends catching up after years of not seeing one another. The party was on cruise control and Timkin thought—as he did every year at around this point—that he could just up and leave and the party would take care of itself. They wouldn't even know he'd left.

He held up his hands like a camera lens and looked around. If you wanted a photograph or a movie scene about New Yorkers in the new millennium, you could do worse than to shoot this group, he thought.

"What are you doing?" Mr. Svenvold asked him.

"I'm thinking of my father," he said, which wasn't true until he said it. "And that little Instamatic he used to bring out."

"I miss him," Mr. Svenvold said. "You know how far we go back."

Mr. Svenvold's eyes went glassy just then, and Timkin saw that he wanted to talk about Timkin's father, which Timkin wasn't anxious to do. He wondered how his parents would take the news of Amy's leaving, but even as he wondered this, he kept glancing at the door to see if one of the new faces coming in was Amy's. The doorman buzzed up.

Timkin listened to the intercom.

"I've got a group of young guys here that say they know you."

"What are their names?"

"Robert, and Jason, and some of their friends."

They were students of his, whom Timkin had told about the balloon block. He told the doorman to let them up.

"*We can only stay* a few minutes," Robert, who was dressed in a thrift shop tuxedo, said as he entered.

"Stay as long as you like," Timkin said, magnanimously.

Now someone put on Timkin's favorite John Coltrane CD, and Timkin got pulled into a conversation with three of his friends from an old job, about a colleague who monopolized the one office bathroom. Timkin nodded as someone spoke; he had no opinion on the subject.

Groups of the guests went downstairs to see the balloons up close and Timkin decided to go with them. He put Lilia in charge of the party while he was gone. And then he walked downstairs and out into the crowds.

There must have been five thousand people milling around, wrapped in furs or long overcoats, or ski parkas, or leather jackets, high school and college kids, and heavily champagned sixty-year-olds, linking arms and singing. Timkin thought then of what a good place it would be for a terrorist to strike, how many prosperous lives could go up in flames. Lots of kids and lots of adults acting like kids, calling out to one another and sipping from flasks. Timkin felt almost happy. And somehow because he was doing this he thought something good might happen. He missed Amy and he felt as though he'd figured out their problems. If she came back, he would know how to do it differently—he himself would be different—and it would work.

They would have children before too long and this whole party would mean something else. Wherever she was he knew she was thinking of him. How could she not? This was their night.

The air had chilled and he could see his breath. He realized he didn't really know the group he was out on the street with. They were the friends of Jordan, and Jordan was here, but Timkin had never really liked Jordan that much. He thought Jordan was spiteful and shallow and possibly an alcoholic.

He thought he recognized some of the faces he passed; a few were people who'd grown up in the neighborhood, including a girl named Tara Feinberg he'd had a crush on. "Hey!" she said. "How are you?"

"Great," he said and she said the same, and he kept saying that to everyone who asked, "Great" and "Can't complain." He glanced up at his apartment window and saw the darkened silhouettes of people moving within, touching arms, listening to stories, eating, and laughing. It made him think of store mannequins enacting scenes in the windows of Saks and Barneys. Were they any less lifelike? He was becoming scornful, he thought. And this was not a scornful night, although he kept picturing someone pouring gasoline on one of the balloons and setting it on fire.

Back upstairs he had another scotch, and soon after that a glass of wine. Not so much because he needed or wanted them, but because they gave him things to do other than to get into a long conversation, which he felt would eventually bring him back to Amy.

When he was a boy, Timkin would go out at midnight in his pajamas to see the balloons. His favorite was always Underdog, because he identified with him, and decades later, at the end of these parties, he would call Amy Polly Purebred (Underdog's bitch, Amy liked to say) and she would play along. She liked Timkin's friends and they, for the most part, took to her, other than

Lilia, who told Timkin once that she didn't trust Amy, that she thought Amy would fool around on Timkin someday.

He looked over now to Lilia and she waved to him and returned to her conversation.

Timkin's mother called at 11:30 to ask how everyone was, and Timkin held the phone out to the room so she could hear the party's chatter.

"What is Amy wearing this year?" she asked.

Timkin described one of Amy's cocktail dresses, a slinky, bare-backed number he'd bought her before a New Year's party at the River Café.

"I'm so glad you're living there, that someone's putting that place to such good use."

Sabrina Willis asked Timkin, "Which Marriott?" She had called one and they hadn't had an Amy Timkin registered there.

"I thought it was the Marriott," he said.

"Let's call her cell phone."

"I already did," Timkin said. "She was going to sleep. She had a long day."

"Oh, she'll talk to us. I'm calling."

"Don't," Timkin said a bit too forcefully. "I mean I promised Amy we'd let her sleep."

Sabrina shrugged.

"I miss her. Would you tell her that I missed her?"

"I will," Timkin said.

And then Sabrina went and joined her husband in the kitchen.

* * *

There were now, he guessed, a hundred and thirty people in his apartment. It might have been the best party he'd given. It was cold out and the mulled cider had been a good idea, and people had had a lot to drink, but not so much that anything out of control was likely to happen.

Buzzed himself and feeling flushed, Timkin moved from circle to circle, freshening glasses, making introductions, greeting utter strangers who were arriving now in significant numbers. He'd ask the lot of them to leave at around two or maybe three if it was still going strong. Who knew when or if this would ever happen again? It reminded him of an Irish wake—a celebration at a time of loss, though he wasn't ready to say yet that he'd lost anything.

Someone reached around and hugged him then from behind.

Amy, he thought, just as he'd wanted, as he'd been imagining all night. The grip was tight and had all of the affection and penitence he had anticipated from her.

But it was Lilia. "What's up?" he said, and she held his glance for too long.

"I know," she said.

"You know?"

"I'm not blind."

"She'll be here tomorrow," Timkin said.

Lilia smiled sadly.

"It's true, you know," he said, still believing it.

"*Fuck* her."

"I'm drunk," Timkin said proudly.

"As you should be."

Someone pushed the music louder. The dining room table got cleared off to the side and around a dozen people were dancing. The lights dropped. A woman in a tight lavender dress whispered something into the ear of a faintly bearded man in a crisp white dress shirt. People filled every room in the apartment—the kitchen, the bedrooms, and the hallways. Strangers would sleep together tonight, he thought; maybe someone was falling in love. Timkin pictured Amy out on the street looking up at their window. Would she have any idea what was happening inside? Would she know what she was missing? Would she see all that was still possible?

It felt like the moment in a movie before something terrible occurred, before the iceberg or the rogue wave.

If I could only stop the film right here, he thought. He took a deep breath and let the spinning room and Lilia's solicitous face settle before his eyes.

"You know what she told me once?"

"What?"

"She told me once she almost didn't marry you; that what it came down to more or less was how much she loved this apartment."

"That's bullshit."

She leaned in and kissed him and Timkin pulled away, as if from a flame.

He refused to believe Amy would ever say anything so unkind. His love for her was his insulation against whatever bad news the world had in store for him.

He stood now at the center of the dance floor, at the center of his party and soaked it all in, all the love and laughter. He closed his eyes, and when he opened them again, his guests were all looking his way. He could see everyone from everywhere: his childhood friends, and his high school teachers, his colleagues from work and people he had liked and admired, or secretly feared. They were all here, and likely Amy was here somewhere as well. That was the nature of the night—you could see your entire past all at once and you could figure out who you were and what it all added up to.

Timkin took a long sip of what he hoped was his own drink, then held the glass aloft. Someone cut the music; they were waiting for the host to speak.

"To Amy!" he called out to everyone he could see. "To Amy!" a chorus of them yelled back, and if this was only the start of the darkest part of his life, Timkin marveled at what he'd already been able to make of it.

HER WORDS

My son, Rajiv, is sleeping with a student from my Dante class. I had made the poor decision of inviting the twelve of them to my house—always perilous—always the chance of someone stumbling on an old letter or journal entry, or some embarrassing laundry or rotted piece of fruit in the refrigerator. And then my son started talking to Rachel Weisman, the slender, dark-haired junior from Santa Barbara, California, with the forthright eyes and the full-lipped mouth, who'd been three times to my office hours. And as I chatted with the rest of the class I kept the two of them in the corner of my awareness. My son has a lot of what I wished for when I was a young man growing up in Bombay. He is well read, and well bred to a point. He is a winning conversationalist, and there are friends of mine who can't believe the eloquent sentences that come forth from his lips, on literature or politics—at that age. "What sort of food do you feed him?" my colleague Jan McAdam asked me. Which had to do, I can only presume, with Jan's own overheated feelings for Rajiv. So I might have been wiser to have my class over—if I was to have them over—on a night when my son was out at a baseball game (though he doesn't go to ball games), or at the alternative newspaper where he serves as arts editor, or at the movies. But one thing led to another, as things do, and he was, well, sleeping with this girl.

They became an item, which puts me in a difficult position, as you might imagine. It isn't that I have another in mind for him, or that I believe he has made a poor choice. It's just that—here's the issue—each day when I walked in the classroom to teach, I had to pretend that I hadn't just seen this Rachel Weisman walking from the shower in just a towel, her long hair wet, and her shoulders gleaming with little beads of water on them, and I had to pretend Rachel Weisman hadn't spent the night within my walls, and that I hadn't heard my son and Rachel Weisman making love, which I did, though I sometimes covered my head with two pillows nearly to the point of suffocation.

I am not stuffy or uptight about these matters. We are in America after all, and this sort of activity goes on. Remember, if you will, that I am in the position of grading her. There are no rules against this, but there probably should be. Our house is relatively small, which compounds the problem. At first she was like a ghost I caught only traces of but never directly encountered. But that began to change, and she became increasingly brazen. After two weeks of their sleepovers, I was reading in bed, which is one of my greatest pleasures, and I'd forgotten to close the door and when I looked up at the entryway, Rachel Weisman was standing there watching me. She had on one of Rajiv's V-neck undershirts and a wraparound skirt worn low enough to expose the black waistband of her underwear, which I did not care to see. Her hair was tied back behind her head, her pale freckled arms folded before her.

"Good book?" she said.

"Yes," I said.

"What is it?"

"Why do you ask?"

"Just curious."

"It's a biography. Of Lawrence."

She seemed to be taking in this information and deciding something.

"I like Lawrence," she said.

Her expressions were at once self-assured and desirous of affirmation. She had lived more than I knew, she seemed to be saying. I feared she was looking at my thinning hair, or the birthmark below my right eye that strangers often mistook for a terrible burn.

"Especially the stories," she said.

"Well, good night then," I said, and in my own house I gently closed my door.

When she saw me in the hallways at school, she would stop me to ask personal things such as, "Did you sleep okay, Mr. Singh?" Or "How'd you like the veggie calzone?"

Once, after class and within earshot of another student, she commented that the heat had stopped working halfway through the night, and she had nearly frozen in the too-thin quilt.

I took her aside. "Do you know how that sounds?" I asked. And she smiled, conspiratorially, as though we two were putting one over on everyone else. "I get it," she said, but I only felt worse.

* * *

A few nights later I told Rajiv that I didn't mind them dating, though I did, but that I'd prefer it if she didn't sleep over. "As *if*," he said. "It's my house too."

My son had begun in the last year to wear modish sideburns, as well as a cluster of beads along a leather strap tied around his neck, like an insouciant surfer, though we live more than two hundred miles from the nearest beach. His T-shirt had a picture of a chimpanzee with President Bush's face.

"But I'm her teacher," I said.

"So."

"You don't see anything strange about that?"

"Not really."

It is at times like this that I wonder if it is possible to dislike your offspring, whether the rule about love holds for every father and son. Because I do not like his selfishness when it comes to me.

The fact that his mother and I have been separated for two years now has made me more pliable and then more resentful. It used to be that I set rules and enforced them. Here I've let him dictate matters, and so the matter of Rachel Weisman has been closed. She will sleep in our house and I will be uncomfortable.

The next thing that happened was that Rachel started missing classes. She's very smart, but she'd miss a class and she'd make an excuse but where she'd been was at my house, in bed with my son.

I can't say for sure they were in bed, but I'd bet good money on it. I would bet one of our cars on it, the six-year-old Volvo. I wondered what the other students thought, and what they knew.

After five missed classes, I told Rachel at dinner she was in danger of failing. And she said she would return, she'd been sick, and she had been working hard on her midterm paper.

"It's really good," my son said. "It's one of the best papers I've ever read."

"I won't miss another class," she said, but then she giggled, because my son must have pinched her under the table. She was dressed in a football shirt I'd passed down to Rajiv.

"If you miss many more, I'll have no choice," I said.

"I won't miss one," she said.

"Tough guy," my son said, when Rachel carried their dishes into the kitchen.

Every once in a while we have these cowboy confrontations.

"Try me," I said.

"I just might," he said.

"What's this about?" Rachel said as she walked back in the room.

Rajiv apologized to me later that night. He said he agreed it was unorthodox. He hadn't planned on dating one of my students, but then I was the one who'd invited them all over. And he had been lonely before that. I told him that surprised me, but it shouldn't have. Away from view, Rajiv could be introverted and remote, as I too had been at twenty-three, though he masks this publicly with his brash defiance.

There was a chance down the line he and Rachel Weisman might want to get an apartment together, he said, and "give this thing a try."

I think he imagined that would comfort me, but it had the opposite effect. Now in class I was having trouble concentrating on anything other than Rachel Weisman. The other students must have picked this up. I rarely made eye contact with Rachel and hardly ever called on her even though she raised her hand more than anyone else. When she spoke I addressed my response to the class as a whole. In retrospect this was both unkind and stupid because it didn't hide anything and rather made our relationship seem like something it wasn't.

One day after class I saw her walk off into the woods behind school with another boy from my class. I became jealous on behalf of Rajiv.

The next class I asked both of them many questions to see if she'd done the reading. She had, but not carefully. I exposed the gaps in her knowledge, and each time I could see her growing angrier, and I thought my son would probably hear about this.

I chose not to care. But I did begin to feel as though I were in the middle of a complicated love affair, and indeed one night I dreamt that she was sleeping in my bed and that my son was teaching and that I was another student in my son's class. I began to have other erotic dreams about Rachel Weisman, and I stopped calling on her altogether, or even acknowledging her existence. At home I mostly ignored her as well and this made her visibly upset. One day as I walked to my car I was aware of her watching me, following me, though I never turned to look. As I drove off I thought I heard someone say, "*Dick*," though it might have been my imagination.

During these weeks I felt volatile in the manner of a hormonally ravaged adolescent. I became acutely aware of every action that occurred in my house, all the arrivals and departures, movie rentals, and book borrowing from my library, the extra garments in Rajiv's closet and the hair and makeup items in the bathroom that made me unbearably nostalgic for the presence of a woman, the hushed and cheerless late-night phone conversations to a female voice in a distant time zone (805 area code), the in-room meals and showers and lovemaking, of which there was decidedly less these days. I wondered whether Rachel had a house key and so to test that fact I double bolted the pantry door—Rachel's entryway of choice—one night when she was studying late at the library, then an hour later unbolted it to avoid seeming childish.

I sensed (or was I hoping?) there was some friction between Rachel and Rajiv, though I never observed any cross words between them, and twice heard them talk about wanting to get their own apartment where they could have some privacy.

On the day before spring break, she handed me a paper on Canto 5 of *The Inferno.* I had taken a stack of papers over to the dark and woody café a block north of the campus where I like to go to hide away from the world. The first seven or eight essays I read were indistinguishable, each with a glimmer or two of earnest intelligence, but predominated by overbaked platitudes. When I got to Rachel Weisman's paper, I began to slow down to the point where I was rereading for the sheer pleasure of encountering her words again. The ideas were exciting, and the sentences exceedingly lucid, even mesmerizing. It didn't matter to me that it was substantially shorter than what I'd asked for. I actually preferred it. I read a few of the paragraphs aloud, and then it struck me that something was off about them.

At first I couldn't tell what, and then I recognized that Rajiv had written the paper. It was in his vocabulary, and it reflected closely his thinking. But then I considered, Wasn't it perfectly possible and even likely for them to talk about the subject? And wouldn't she hear some of his ideas and agree with them, and then be unable to avoid them for purposes of forming her own thesis?

I simply heard Rajiv's tenor voice as I read it, and when I tried to hear hers, the voice wouldn't come forth. I considered simply asking her to write a different paper, but her response, I knew, would be justifiable outrage. They would both hate me.

The bottom line is I accepted Rachel's paper, but I only gave her a B. She stormed—or maybe just walked—into my office saying she'd never once in her life gotten a B for a grade; that her worse mark had been a B+. I said: "There's always a *first* time, isn't there?"

Somehow that came out more, well, *sexual* than I wanted it to, and I realized that we were standing quite close at the time, and I backed away.

She was studying my birthmark again, or maybe my eyes.

"He's right about you, isn't he?" Rachel said.

She held her mouth in an ill-mannered smirk.

I said, No, Rajiv wasn't likely to be right about me. There was much about me my son didn't know but that was not a conversation I felt like having with a student. The paper was good but I had questions as to its authenticity, I said. She could write an addendum, or she could write a paper on how she'd arrived at her ideas, and I'd certainly have a look.

I thought that afternoon and evening about that line—*He's right about you.* And I tried to think of what that might mean. I have never done anything to compromise my position as tenured professor at a first-rate liberal arts college. And even if I had, I couldn't imagine why my son would report such a thing.

I began to believe that Rachel might bring the matter up

with a dean and so I mentally prepared for such a confrontation.

Had my door been ajar?

"It was," I said in practice.

Did I have any burning reasons for questioning the authenticity of the paper, and was there any reason I had to stand virtually on top of her while I had been having this discussion?

"I wasn't on top of her, and the paper simply didn't sound like her."

And how was it that she knew so much about the inside of my home?

"What did she say about it?"

"What did you mean by there's always a first time?" the dean would ask me.

"We were talking of her grade," I would say.

"You were flirting with her while you were talking of her grade?"

"She's sleeping with my son," I would say.

"Well, how did that happen?" he would then ask, and I'd have to say, "They met at my house."

"Did it occur to you that that wasn't a good idea?"

"How can you stop a couple of horny kids?"

I actually said this aloud.

"It would be best if you refrained from describing a student under your supervision as *horny*," the dean would say.

"I've done nothing," I'd say, but neither of us would believe that was true.

But it never came to that. Ultimately I gave her an A.

Rachel stopped by my room the night after I'd changed her grade, again while I was reading in bed. I had on my pajamas and a robe.

"What the hell was that for?" she said, which is a fairly inappropriate way to talk to your professor. "I didn't deserve an A."

She was out of breath and jittery. My son was working late at the newspaper.

"I'd rather not have this conversation in my bedroom if that's okay, and anyhow I thought you said you deserved an A?"

"I deserved an A minus," she said. "I only want what I deserve."

"You're getting an A."

"There were no comments on it."

I noticed that one of her bottom teeth was chipped, her eyes moist and reddened. I wondered about her mental health.

"Your grade was my comment," I said.

She shook her head in disgust.

"That's so typical of you."

"What do you know about me? How do you know what's typical?" I tried to relax my face; to understand that the world didn't need to fall apart, but it felt like it was, all my rage and sadness surrounding the divorce, and my problems at the college, and the neighbors had converged within me. "None of this is *typical*."

She was too close to me right then. I wanted her to leave. I wanted my son to get back home.

"I bet I remind you of her," she said.

"Who?"

"Why did she leave you anyhow?"

"What are you talking about?"

She smiled cruelly. "I bet I know."

"I'd rather not hear your theories, Ms. Weisman. They're not original enough, and in fact I'd rather if you didn't continue to live here with us. This isn't how I'd like to live."

"Such passion. Such *unbridled warmth*."

"I've got a lot of warmth for those in my life who merit it, but I've really had enough of this if that's okay with you."

She looked angry, and then sad.

"You know, Mr. Singh . . . I really don't like it when you ignore me in class. It's very cruel. And it's really not fair. I'm a good student, one of your best. I tried for two years to get into your course, you know. It isn't fair to ignore me."

"Did you write it?" I asked. "Tell me the truth."

"Who cares?"

"I do for one. The university does for another. You know you can get kicked out for something like this."

She shook her head in exasperation.

"Of course I wrote it. He never even read it. He just made a big deal about it because he wanted you to take an interest."

We didn't see Rachel for two weeks after that, not at home anyhow. She sat in the back of class and never raised her hand. She did all the work, and she left immediately afterward. She and Rajiv were in a holding pattern for now, trying to figure out what was next.

He didn't hold me responsible, he said. They had their own issues. I felt as though I'd destroyed something, but at the same time I felt as though a burden had been lifted.

A week before the end of school the dean—the one I'd imagined Rachel speaking to—stopped into my office to say that Rachel Weisman was going back to California. She wanted to send her final paper in from there. And she would do any homework I requested but her father had died, and she wanted to be with her mother, the dean said. Her father's health had been deteriorating for a long time. He'd had two strokes, the last one incapacitating. He'd been a sculptor and photographer, and they'd had a rocky relationship. This last part Rajiv told me.

"She will have the whole summer as her deadline," I said, and the dean nodded grimly, and somewhat paternally. I wondered if he had more to say, but he didn't and without further incident took his leave.

That night as I parked my car and sat outside my house, I thought about how distant Rajiv and I had become. How much I'd wanted everything to be different. He was a gifted boy. Bold in ways I once was. I was immensely proud of him, so much that I imagined he'd written something he might not yet be capable of. Perhaps it was my vanity that screwed all of this up. It would be untrue to say that I never looked at Rachel in the wrong way. And even now a part of me hopes that I'll see her in her towel leaving the shower, her damp hair falling lushly down her back. It reminds me of a period in my life in which I wouldn't have cared what my own father said or thought. I would have done what I wanted in the name of love.

HOWLING AT THE MOON

W*e sat on the screened-in porch* of my new family's sum-merhouse, passing bottles of red wine and telling death stories. I was twelve and wasn't drinking.

Charles had a friend whose cousin lost his ear to a wolf, then froze in a blizzard. He'd been spring camping on Mount Hood in Oregon and hadn't planned for snow.

"He was iced solid . . . curled up like a fetus," Charles said. "Took them four days to find him. He bandaged that poor ear to his head with a handkerchief and duct tape."

"I know that mountain. You can't trust it," Walt said. He was puffy and pale in the candlelight and expertly rolled his own cigarette as he spoke. Behind him a hundred yards away, I saw a single lit window in the house's back wing where I guessed my mother and their father, Norman, were having a late supper alone, away from us.

Deborah said when she was ten, she watched camp counsel-ors pull a drowned girl from a lake in Switzerland. The girl had slipped out of sight, away from the roped-in swimming area, and she'd hit her head against a rock.

"They gave her mouth-to-mouth, but looking at her you can tell she was gone," Deborah said. She dipped her finger into a pool of wax at the candle's base and then let the hot liquid slide across her palm before hardening.

"That was the only dead body I ever saw," she said, and she spoke toward me. Everyone else, I guessed, had heard this before. "I kept thinking 'That could have been me.' Absolutely."

Walt said he saw a football player sever his spine during a game; the boy never heard the linebacker behind him. And on Nan's way onto a train in Calcutta, she said, she nearly tripped over a corpse before realizing what it was.

At my turn, I told them about watching my brother die in a car accident. He was thirteen years old at the time and I was nine.

"My mother was driving home from the lake and I kicked a pile of tennis balls around her seat to the front," I said. "They rolled beneath her feet and she smashed the car."

I told them more, about the ride to the hospital, and the waiting: the dismal yellow waiting room, my mother on a separate bench, rubbing her hands over her pant legs rocking forward and back, lips moving, blaming me, I thought. She's never stated this, but even now, twenty-two years later, I can't see how she wouldn't want to shift the burden. How she wouldn't tell herself she was driving safely and nothing would have happened had I followed the car rules. I would understand that.

"Shit, Lou," Walt said. "No one told us. No one said a thing."

They stared over as if a person had taken my place on the porch. Nan reached her arm around me and held me tight. No one asked me anything else.

* * *

That was the summer Mother and Norman had decided to test us all as a family: four weeks in Norman's summer home off the coast of Maine. He and my mother weren't officially engaged, but the subject was in the air.

My new brothers and sisters were in college or older; I didn't know their ages exactly, but again and again I'd heard about their lives. In the stories my mother told, they soared untethered, like people in magazines or movies. They weren't like anyone I knew. They'd driven motorcycles in foreign countries, won grants and awards, performed onstage or in the living rooms of glamorous apartments. My mother saved newspaper clippings about them. "They're all creative," she said on the trip from Auburn, New York, to Maine. She spoke as though they were already hers.

"Charles is the painter. Remember?" she said. "He had a show of some sort in SoHo? I told you about it. Nan's the sculptor; Walt plays in the jazz band. Deborah is the actress; she's been in two films."

Deborah had a small role in a movie we saw last Christmas, my mother said. The closest one to my age, Lauren, was studying in France. As an artist, she hadn't defined herself, my mother said, "But she writes nicely. Like you, she's got a good sense for people."

In Lauren's room, where they put me, there were piles of letters, diaries, and typed short stories, "The One-Eyed Jack," "Lantern Night," "Late Show," "The Tall Man with the Purple Felt Hat." Mostly, though, there were pictures. They lined shelves, covered corkboard: collages of the family in faded beachwear or thick, wooly sweaters, heads gazing forward over their folded arms, wild hair whipping back in the wind, on the boats, on the beaches, groups of them touring museums, walking narrow city streets, picking mussels in the fog. I tried to imagine my mother and me in those scenes on the walls. I felt as if something had passed us by.

Lauren's bedcovers were white goose down and the floors were dark lacquered wood. On the blue night table was a photo album with handwritten captions about people. "Me and Nan in Paris," "Charles after the ski trip . . ." "Bongs Away!"

When the house was empty, I dug around like an archaeologist. I raked over the CDs, the photo albums stacked in the corners, and flipped through the yearbooks, reading the inscriptions. On a bureau top there were pictures of Lauren in shorts and in a bathing suit, her legs tawny and long. It was strange to think of her as a relative; I looked at pictures of my new sister and I was hypnotized. It didn't feel right and in many ways I was glad she wasn't with us that month. I didn't know how I would act. It's a funny thing to meet a group of people older than you and be told that they are your family, you will live with them and not hate them or ignore them or fall in love with them. I stayed up late one night studying Lauren's clothes and desk drawers and books. I found her diary and I read a few pages. What I read embarrassed me; it was about her and a boy in a field at night. I looked at her in a photograph and then at the boy in her album. I imagined them behind some trees in a darkened glen. I searched through her clothes for what she might have worn that night and settled on a thick gray sweatshirt, crossed oars on the chest, paint and grass stains flecked across the back. I threw it in my bag under my windbreaker.

* * *

For a while after my brother, Tim, died, my mother slept in his room, in his bed with the Buffalo Bills sheets. She kept his posters and papers and model warplanes intact. About a year later she moved back into her own bedroom and began throwing those things out. She swept through the house like a wind, cleaning, clearing, and rearranging. She said crisis was something you could turn around, you could make something positive out of it.

One time, while I was asleep, she put all our photo albums and my brother's things in cardboard crates and carried them to the curb. She pulled the curtains from the window in his room, so sun would shine in always. She made the room her den. She went back to school for her master's degree. She rode her bike to class and carried her book bag over her shoulders. In addition she took yoga, then tai chi. Early mornings when I looked out the window, I could see my mother crouching low, arms leveling out as if sliding across an imperceptible surface. She'd spend hours in the attic sculpting naked figurines, and then she painted our house with the same energy, inside and out.

When Tim and I were little, my mother forced her way into a group of fathers who organized Scout trips and fishing weekends. "I'm their father and their mother," she said. She took Tim and me to football games and karate movies and professional wrestling and she feigned interest until we told her we didn't like them, and then she found other things for us to do. We quit Scouts and went on our own trips. My mother consulted a field guidebook that showed how to coax a fire, how to pick edible berries and avoid the poisonous ones.

One time, under the full moon, she taught us how to howl like wolves. We'd pitched camp illegally at a lakeside summer camp a half hour outside of town, but the season had ended and there were no cars parked in the spaces behind the cabins or at the foot of the slate gray mess hall.

"Point your lips straight out like this," she said, and from the side she looked, I remember, like a fish. "Oooooooo," we moaned.

"That's it. Now like someone's dropped a box on your foot. Oowwww! Wooooooooooo. Put them together."

"Jeez. We know what a howl sounds like," Tim said. I swung my fist down hard on his foot and he elbowed me harder in the arm. "Oowwww," we both yelled.

And my mother answered, "Wooooooooooo."

Long after my mother went to sleep, we didn't let up. We howled for hours until our throats were hoarse and our eyes burned for want of sleep. Tim's howl was loudest and sounded like a moose call. Our joke was that there were moose heading across the lake from Canada because of Tim's howl.

After Tim died, I had a dream we were camping, the three of us crammed into our tent along the lake. We'd zip the sleeping bags together, and our heads lay in a line, like bowling balls on a rack. We glanced over at one another or stared straight up at the roof of the tent, listening for bears or moose or a wolf. We heard them and saw their shadows run along the outside of the tent. They whined and growled and they poked shapes into the pea green fabric. But we kept them out with our voices. When I awoke once from that dream, I walked the house for signs of him. I stepped into his room and saw my mother there and we looked at each other with the same face of disappointment and I knew that she'd heard him in my steps, or seen him in the shadows I threw on the walls before I walked through the door.

* * *

Two winters after the accident, my mother took cross-country ski lessons. She saved her money and went for a ski weekend in Stowe, Vermont, with four of her classmates. They stayed at the von Trapp family lodge, the place the *Sound of Music* family moved to, and it was there that she met Norman.

He came to our house six or seven times after that for weekends or short vacations, but he never seemed at ease. Ours is a depressed area even by upstate standards. He made promises to us when he walked through the living and dining room—about couches and tables he'd buy for us, and trips he'd take us on. He praised the simplicity of our town but he meant something else. He meant it was no place to live.

The day we arrived in Maine, my mother and Norman disappeared into what they called the adult house, really just a separate wing with its own entryway. I saw them for short snatches in the mornings or before I went to sleep, but during the first two weeks I think I had only one meal with my mother. She and Norman took long trips on Norman's boat and went out for dinner. Sometimes I'd run into my mother in the morning on a walk and we'd look at each other surprised, like former neighbors glancing at each other across a restaurant floor, friends that had neglected to call each other or stay in touch. She would say, "I'm sorry, but Norman and I need this time together, to get to know each other. It's very important."

Everyone had a routine. Charles set his easel up in the living room at sunrise and painted watercolors of schooners, yachts, and lobster skiffs. He blasted the Beastie Boys while he worked, and by one he'd finished. Walt squalled sax for hours in his room, but never before noon. His eyes were vein red and his room smelled like cigarettes. He taught me how to play a few notes but his mouthpiece tasted ashy, and my stomach pitched. Around sunset, Deborah read scripts in the big back bedroom with the light violet walls. I could hear her alter her voice, crying, laughing, or rattling in anger. Twice I read parts with her and watched her forget for a while who I was. Nan stripped furniture on the porch in those late hours and sometimes when I helped her we could hear Deborah soliloquizing through the window.

If I was ever noticeably alone for too long, someone would sit beside me. They took turns taking me for walks.

One morning, when I'd been watching him paint, helping him mix colors and clean his brushes, Charles told me I was on an island and I needed a pair of big shorts. The ones I was wearing were too tight. He ran with me down the upstairs hall to a closet piled high with old clothes. He dug his head in like a wino leaning into a Dumpster and he handed me two pairs of shorts.

"Try these on," he said.

I squeezed out of the shorts I had on and into the baggy pair he'd handed me. The legs were down almost to my knees and spread out like sails. The waist was loose, but Charles pulled a strap on the side and it contracted. He smiled. They were just like his.

"We've got tons more where that came from," he said, and I could see it was true. There were old jerseys, lacrosse shirts, rugby sweaters, clothes I'd seen in a picture on Lauren's walls.

"I've got T-shirts," I said. "I don't need any more." I had one of Lauren's on that said CALIFORNIA with a picture of a wave.

"Well, they're here if you want them. They're right in the closet there and you can take whatever you want."

When he left, I picked out an old gray shirt that said PROPERTY OF DARTMOUTH ATHLETIC DEPARTMENT. I liked the idea of belonging to an athletic department. It seemed like an honor, a sign you'd caught the passes or done the required push-ups. I carried the shirt and shorts to Lauren's room and slipped them into my bag.

I was in the bathroom washing my face when I heard muffled voices from Nan and Deborah's room, then laughs, a room full of laughs. Everyone was in that room. I walked to the doorway.

Walt and Deborah were under the covers in one bed, Nan was in the other fixing a cassette tape with a pencil. There were bags of Oreos and bottles of pop strewn about and serious books, opened on their spines, then abandoned. A music box sat on the nightstand surrounded by tapes separated from their cases. Charles was flitting about the room imitating someone.

I watched this scene for a while and for a moment I imagined Tim telling the story. He would be near Charles's age and I would be sitting there listening.

The woman Charles mimicked was someone he'd waited on the night before, someone he spilled wine on. She wanted Charles fired. She told him she would write a letter to the owner of the restaurant about Charles's ineptitude.

"Oh, there's *nothing* you can do now. Not *now*," he said in a mock falsetto.

Charles said he offered to buy a new shirt and to give the couple their meal on the house. The woman said that wasn't the point. The shirt was from Indonesia and it was irreplaceable.

He told the woman to try cold water and salt. "Oh, what's the use?" she said. "What the hell is the use?"

I saw Nan glance at me. I felt I was peering through someone's window.

"How long have you been there, Lou?" she said. Then everyone looked at me.

"Just a couple of seconds."

"Well, get your butt in here," Walt said. "We need some new discourse. The air's getting stale in here." He nodded his head toward Charles.

I felt this was a cue for me to speak, to say something interesting or fresh, but I couldn't think of anything to say. I felt disconnected. The fog outside was so thick I could imagine it rolling into the house, filling it completely like cotton in a bottle.

"Crummy day out, huh?" I said.

"I love days like this," Nan said. "These are my favorite days."

"I'm with you, Lou," Walt said. "I hate this shit. Look out there. You can't see ten feet."

"Why do you need to?" Nan asked. "For a few days the world is a ten-foot bubble in front of you."

I thought about walking around the island in a bubble, passing cars for a moment, then horses and dogs. I'd walk to the other side to the beach, seeing the sand only when it sprung from between my bare toes.

"Are you worried about what's going to happen to you?" Deborah asked.

I said, "Yes, I am worried."

Deborah laughed and then hushed herself. "I'm sorry, Lou," she said. "I was asking Charles."

That night I sat up late reading Lauren's diary, the white quilt covering me in the cool damp room. I was beyond the sex scene to the day after and Lauren was filled with regret and angst. The boy had called her three times and she wouldn't come to the phone.

Everyone was to tell the guy she was out, or sleeping or gone for a run. She was confused by her feelings. She said she wanted to die or curl away for a month or so. She lay for hours in bed—this bed, under these covers, and sipped from a bottle of Bénédictine. I felt as though she was confessing to me, that it was just the two of us up late talking in her room and no one else could hear. I would tell her things. I would tell her about the accident. About Tim and my mother.

He was in eighth grade when he died. I was in fourth. To this day I do not remember resenting him, or envying him, or whispering beneath my breath or to anyone else that I wanted him killed. I believed I kicked the balls to spite my mother although I cannot remember why. That she would slip harder onto the accelerator and lose her steering, that she would brake too hard so the car would whir, like a loosed top, off the road into a tree, were not things I could have imagined. That I would see my brother twisted ghastly, suspended like a night-blinded bird in broken glass, was something I could not have dreamed.

My father had been gone since I was three, dead of a heart attack. But my mother said the sadness that she felt then was nothing like what she felt when Tim died.

For a few months we both saw counselors but we did not talk about that day or my brother. It was as though we had lost our history, as if time started the day after the crash. The counselor said we should have had a mourning period together, a time in which we could just sit and think of Tim and be sad. It was absolutely the healthiest thing to do, he said, to vocalize, to mourn out loud. It never came about.

Instead my mother joined a support group of people who lost sons or daughters and she began having friends from the group over for dinners and small parties that would end long after I'd gone to bed. One night, when she'd had a good deal to drink, she crawled next to me in my bed and smiling, I could see this in the half-light, told me I was her whole life, "kit and kaboodle," and though she'd meant it as a gesture of intimacy, there was something false in that moment that made her seem distant as the stars from me and altogether unknowable.

I read more of the diary. There were other boys. One Lauren slept with at his house. His parents were away in California, so they set up a tent with sleeping bags on the front lawn. He chewed tobacco and kept a cup for spitting in the tent. Another one she danced with until six in a dorm room at his college.

I looked again at Lauren's picture. I walked to the closet. I tried on one of her skirts and then I put her red sweater on over that. I was twelve then and knew this was the most intimate I would get with a girl six years older. I stood in front of the mirror and turned side to side. I ran my hands up the front of the sweater and down my sides, over my ribs and hips. I looked ridiculous. I ran to check the door, to see if it was locked. I flipped the radio on and I danced, the skirt swirling around me. Then I lifted the sweater off slowly, dangling it over the bed. The shades on my window were open, so I turned the lamp off and let the moonlight stream in. I slid the skirt down to my ankles and then kicked it high into the air. It floated like a parachute to the floor across the room. I danced on top of the quilt and the bedsprings shrieked. When my legs gave out, I sank exhausted into the bed and let the music spin the room.

* * *

The things my mother did alone before, she did now with Norman. They ran together. She taught him tai chi. He taught her to drink scotch and champagne—rather than the fruity rum drinks she drank before—although he said she taught him to moderate. They'd begun to gesture alike, share expressions, finish each other's sentences.

"You know what it is about your mother?" Norman would say. And my mother would answer that with something different each day. Norman said he lost thirty pounds and twenty years being around my mother. They talked with and around me for ten minutes or so, asking me how I liked it on the island, whether I could get used to that kind of life, and then they'd disappear somewhere, carrying a blanket, a checkered tablecloth, a wicker picnic basket with wine bottles peeking out.

One time I was on my way over to visit and through their living room window I saw my mother walking on Norman's back. He was agonized. His balding head was bright pink. He was completely naked, his flesh tanned and bundled at the base of his spine. She was in shorts and a T-shirt walking on top of him. She is a tall, strong woman, and, on top of Norman, she filled the room. I stared, fascinated, and then I saw my mother look over for a second. She caught my eye and smiled, a sly and heartless grin that scared the hell out of me. I tore from the window to the gravel road to the grass that ran down the coastline. I ran over wet rocks and seaweed and a long grass field until my face poured sweat and my lungs hurt.

After that I avoided her. I stopped my visits. When I heard her voice in the kids' house, I locked myself in Lauren's room or I escaped out the kitchen door. She left me notes and I didn't respond. If Norman came by alone, to change a lightbulb or check the flower beds, I'd talk to him and try to act normal. I tried to forget my image of him, naked on the floor, grimacing in pain.

They kept to their routines, though. I still saw them in low crouches in the white light of morning. They still took boat trips in the afternoons.

In our last week, the fog had begun to scatter. At noon one morning I woke late and heard Walt playing a sad, dreamy song on the saxophone. I pressed my ear on the wall to hear. My ear vibrated. It surged warmth. I walked that morning to the general store with Charles and Nan. Norman had a charge account at Percy's, and when we walked through the door, Percy jumped to attention as if we were something important.

"What can I do for you, Charlie?" he asked. Behind the glass at the front counter were fresh donuts, glazed and powdered, long twirling crullers and fat Danishes smothered in cheese or fruit, wild cinnamon rolls twirled around like long boa constrictors. And then there were meats: sausages, salamis, hams, and, on the shelf over them, hard crusty rolls and bagels and croissants. Charles pointed and Percy lunged to keep up, piling things with metal tongs into a sack. On the shelves behind Percy were pickled fish and imported crackers, tins of Danish cookies.

Nan had a list out and she filled a cart with vegetables and fruit and fish. Then, as if they were afterthoughts, she dropped boxes and cans into the cart—cereal, crackers, pasta, soup— like the guy who wins fifteen minutes to pull everything off the shelves at the P&C.

"Whatever you want you should get it now, Lou," she said.

"This is our shopping for the week." They charged two cases of beer and four bottles of red wine and asked that everything be delivered.

When I saw my mother and Norman walk through the front door of the store, I ducked back into the freezer room. I waited there in that cold metal box, watching through a crack. I saw Nan talking to them, saw them buy cheese and a loaf of bread, and then I watched them leave. By the time I left the freezer room I was shivering and my lips felt hard and brittle.

At the counter I bought a brownie and I walked with Charles and Nan down the road with it.

In the afternoon it began to rain and music streamed through the house. Walt drank a beer on the porch and I asked him for one.

"Hey," he asked Deborah, "is it cool? Can Lou here have a beer?"

"I don't know," Deborah said. She looked at me from the side of her eye.

"Sounds pretty treacherous. First a beer, then what?"

Walt opened a beer for me.

"Here you go, Skipper," he said.

He sprawled himself atop an old mattress. There were wicker benches and seats in the other corner of the porch, but no one ever sat on them. They were like roped-off museum pieces. Walt was bare chested and he wore what looked like a doctor's green scrub pants. His face was flecked with patches of beard, like a comic book pirate. He sang along to "Wild Horses," his vowels and consonants indistinguishable.

I walked with my beer to the front of the house where Nan rubbed sandpaper over an old desk.

"What's up?" I asked.

"Nothing really, just trying to get some thinking done. Is that a beer?"

"Yup."

She didn't look at me or stop what she was doing.

"What are you thinking about?" I asked.

"Nothing important." Her arm worked fast, as though she were driving something unspeakable out of the desk. I wanted to help her sand. I wanted to think alongside her.

"Can I sand too?" I asked.

"Lou? What's the deal with your mom? What's this all about?" she asked.

When I walked back to the porch, Walt and Deborah had switched from beers to harder stuff and they were saying nasty things about people I didn't know.

The rain had let up a bit so I jogged down the road past Percy's and then walked along the ocean. After a half hour or so, I headed inland through a wooded area, over patches of shrub and vine. Then I cut to the other island.

The downpour began soft and warm and the wind spread over my face. My high-tops filled with water. I decided not to care about anything.

When I made it back to town, I hung out in the video arcade. I played video games, one after another until I'd spent everything in my pocket—sixteen dollars. I played until it was one o'clock and they closed the place down.

* * *

When I arrived back at the house, I heard voices downstairs: Deborah's and a male voice I didn't recognize, a date, I guessed, because there was low jazzy music and the flicker of candles and incense. I sat on the newly varnished stairs awhile listening to the conversation floating through the air like cigarette rings, thoughts unfinished, questions not answered. It didn't seem as if they were talking with each other at all. They were confessing, giving up parts of themselves.

The man talked about a sailing trip he took with eleven people, as part of Outward Bound. They stayed on the boat six days, no cabins or bathrooms.

"We hung our butts over these little white pails. We got to know each other, that's for sure. There was nothing to do except get to know each other. I know a little about everyone on the boat, more than I know about most of my friends."

"No bathrooms," Deborah said, as if making a mental note on a house she might buy. "What did you sleep on?"

"We pulled a tarp over us at night to keep the wind off. There wasn't a lot of room. When we finally got off the boat onto land, we stood for a moment in the shape of the boat. We hadn't gotten used to the larger space."

I could see his shadow pass over the wall teetering up and back.

"Did you fall in love? Did you find yourself?" she asked. "Did you merge with the breach?"

"You're making fun of me. If you want to know, it was like the ark. I mean, there were older people and a few high school kids. We caught our food. Fish for breakfast, lunch, and dinner. I did most of the cleaning and gutting. That was my job. And I found out a lot about myself."

"In a play this summer I played the wife of a policeman who gets killed," Deborah said. "When the play's over each time, I can't snap out of it. It's not that I'm lost in my character. I don't believe in that. It's just that I'm aware at the end of each night that someone had died."

I listened to Deborah and I didn't buy it. It sounded like a lot of crap, that you could summon sadness like that. Or that you could arrive at it for a few nights, as though it were a hotel you stayed in.

Then she told this guy about my brother dying, the whole story. They sat silently a moment after she'd finished.

"He carries this around with him," she said finally. "Can you imagine? It broke my heart."

"My God," he said.

I stayed there on the steps until the conversation started up again, hushed and affectionate. I could see their shadows merge, their voices springing from somewhere offstage, like lines in a puppet show, or growls and whines outside my dream tent.

When I headed back to bed it was 2:30. I thought about what Deborah said. I thought of that policeman as I tried to fall asleep. Though I tried to shut them out, I could still hear them, the clink of glasses being washed, the low murmur of the stereo, the rhythmic rise and fall of their conversation, which curled into the shape of my dreams.

When I opened my eyes again, I saw Lauren leaning over me. She was back early, I thought, and wanted her room. Her diary was opened and she'd probably seen it. I shrank back into my cover. "I can move. I'll move out of here," I said.

But it was my mother's face. I bolted upright and she put her finger over my mouth. "Sssshh," she said, and I could smell scotch on her breath. She smelled sour.

"There's a full moon outside," she said. "Let's go howl at the moon."

"Where's Norman?" I asked.

"Sleeping," she said. "He doesn't do too well after midnight." She lay down next to me and rested her head on her bent arm, like a sleepover friend. She put her hand on my shoulder. I hadn't seen her close-up in four days. Her black hair was tied in a thick braid behind her head, like a teenager's, like the pictures of Lauren.

"I've been talking with Norman about things, Lou," she said. "I've learned a great deal."

"And . . ."

"And he says I've been blaming you. I've been blaming you for everything. You told the kids something the other night."

My head felt hot and still swollen with sleep. I began then to silently cry. I couldn't control the muscles in my face.

She put her hands on either side of me.

"Well, that's not right. It's absolutely not right," she said. She pulled a strand of hair off my face. "It's as wrong as wrong can be," she said, and she kissed my forehead. "Got it?" She kissed it again in the same spot. "Am I getting through?"

"Yes," I said, and she tickled me.

"You were the only thing that kept me from jumping in front of a train. Got it? Do you?" I was twisting from her. Against my will, I laughed. She pressed against me, full weight. My mother is a very strong woman. Her hands were on my wrists, pinning me back.

"Come on, Lou," she said, then raising herself. "It's a beautiful night. The sky is clear now, absolutely clear, and there are a million stars. Let's go howling."

I peered around her, through the window, and I could see she was right. I could see the Big Dipper, Taurus, Orion's Belt. My mother used to tell us stories about the stars.

"All right," I said, and she released me. "Let's go."

I pulled on my blue jeans and a T-shirt that felt cold against my skin. I felt my mother's eyes on me, felt her watching me lace my sneakers. I was startled by the attention, but I knew to take it when I could get it; I wanted her to take notice.

Like cartoon characters, we walked on our toes down the stairs, making exaggerated efforts not to wake anyone, holding fingers over each other's mouths and giggling. She took a blanket from the living room couch and wrapped it around us.

We walked along the gravel road that crested the water and we kicked stones back and forth. Branches of high oaks and maples covered us like a long canopy. The crickets and owls and night birds screeched and I said, "It's a jungle out here." My mother made a sound like an ape, "ooo, ooo, ooo, ooo." She puffed air beneath her lower lip for effect. She laughed. She was giddy.

At the old pier we walked out on the creaking planks and watched the moon shine phosphorescent over the black water. I skipped a flat rock, watched it fly across the sheen, dart about like a fly, then disappear.

My mother spread the blanket out at the end of the pier and we sat on it cross-legged. We were at the end of a wide rocky bay and the land jutted out a quarter mile on the other side. There were a few homes along there. One of them still had a light on.

We leaned our heads back and stared straight up. We made shapes with our minds and explained them to each other point by point, like the Rorschach tests the counselor made me take after the accident. I thought about something my mother told me once—that some of the stars you were looking at had burned to ash a thousand years ago. It dazzled me; that we were watching a galactic past that would never again repeat itself. I thought that if they were watching us right now through some sort of superlens, they'd be watching the Egyptians build the pyramids. Everything had changed. Nothing was like it had been before.

My mother craned her neck at the moon like a flower yearning for light and she howled, slow and mournfully. The sound hung over the water, then repeated itself two hundred yards away.

She did this again, the music of the waves and wind riding beneath her voice. Then she laughed as she'd done when we howled before, but the sound seemed to turn her mouth into something she hadn't expected, thin and startling, as though she'd landed on the wrong key. She leaned over to kiss my cheek and I smelled the scotch.

"We should do this again," she said. "Every full moon."

She ran her hand along my back and I felt myself tense.

"We need to do things like this," she said, as though it was just something to do.

I looked away from her to the water, black as ink. I am thirty-one now, with my own children, and live across the country from my mother and Norman. We see each other only occasionally, but even in a year when we did not speak at all I never felt so far from her as I did right then.

I waited for her hand to drop, then I howled, a long high moan that made my chest burn. I closed my eyes and let the sound carry into the damp night air. I howled for a long while there, her next to me, silent, listening, my ears and throat ringing.

SOMEBODY'S SON

They are both at the door when we walk up, the old lady in a hand-knit green pullover, the man in a gray cardigan that bleeds gray onto his undershirt. He looks just-risen from bed. His voice is hoarse, and he holds his wife's arm as they make their way out to the front stoop. They look us over.

Eddie and I both have gum boots on, jeans, flannel shirts, and down vests. Upstate clothes. Eddie had them first and I followed, not deliberately—item by item—so it snuck up on me that I'd done it. Now here I am looking quite a bit like Eddie.

Eddie introduces us as new in town. True enough. Stopping by just to meet our neighbors, which is a stretch.

"Quite a layout here. What do you have, a hundred fifty, two hundred acres?" Eddie looks around as though searching for a boundary fence, though he already knows the dimensions of this place.

"Three hundred eleven," she says. "All the woods there behind the creek and the hollow there, to the river. Right up to the Oswegatchie there."

"Beautiful river," Eddie says, like he's complimenting her on a watercolor she's made or a turkey she's cooked. "Nice little town too. Pine. Nice place."

The old lady tilts her head meditatively. "I guess it is."

"Bit cold out here," Eddie says. "You mind if we come inside a moment or two?"

Once inside Eddie finagles us tea and biscuits, and he starts playing therapist, nodding his head as the woman, Mrs. Berner, tells us about disasters in her life. She says the land has become a nightmare since her husband's stroke two years back.

Eddie plays slow to agree.

"But you've got a real farm," he says. "That's the way to live, straight from the earth."

"It's too big for us. We haven't been able to do a thing out there for years. It's a waste," she says. "And it's not like we have a pension rolling in. We've got no income."

He's managed to get her to talk him into his pitch.

"You ever thought of selling the place, getting some smaller spot in town?" I ask.

Eddie shoots me a look: slow down. He's training me so I can close this sale later on my own. He sips his tea, then places the cup on the table next to him so he can use his hands to paint the picture.

"What Randall means is that the two of you deserve to be living better," Eddie says. "Lord sakes, you've earned it. What kind of life would you want if you could have anything you've dreamed of?"

"I'd say we've had . . . what we wanted," the old man says, and he looks so pathetic it breaks my heart.

"Think big," Eddie says. "Think of what you'd want if money were no object. I mean for me, I'd think of a new car, a speedboat, maybe a cruise to South America. You ever been to South America?"

The man lets out a sepulchral cough. Then he holds the handkerchief over his mouth and spits.

Eddie switches the conversation, to hunting and fishing, and finding no traction there asks Mrs. Berner about her children.

"Oh, they're in California now," she says.

"Think about visiting them," Eddie says. "It's a beautiful world out there."

"I guess they've grown apart from us."

She seems to want us to ask about this.

"Be nice to have a manageable place in town, don't you think? And a little cash to take care of Mr. Berner," I say.

"Sometimes I think that's just what we need, and then we just can't seem to say so long to this place. You know how that is. You go to sleep and you wake up, and you're still here."

I excuse myself to go to the bathroom. Mrs. Berner points the way and lets me loose in her house.

I think about us sitting there in the Berners' living room and it makes me angry at them. There's no reason to be so trusting in a world like ours. A couple of months ago I read an article about an old couple that let a man into their house supposedly to fix their stove. They didn't even have a problem with their stove, but they trusted him, and when they let him inside, he pulled a pistol on them. He made them lie down on the ground. He took everything they had in the house, and before he left he must have thought they'd had a long enough look at his face because he shot them both dead. I wander through the cold drafty rooms of the Berners' house and I think about us being homicidal maniacs. We're invited guests, in their house, and there's no one around to hear us or see us. No witnesses. And there's plenty here to rob. I sold at an antique shop one summer, and the Berners have possessions lying around that would bring a decent price: old snow globes; a gilded music box, mahogany it looks like; a tall grandfather clock with Westminster chimes and the wrong time, standing in the corner like a forgotten cathedral; a 1950 Winchester 12-gauge in an otherwise empty gun rack; a reading lamp with a silk shade and glass bead fringe. I flick the switch but then I see—there's no bulb. There's beautiful stuff here that doesn't look like it's been touched for years. Would they miss it if it was all gone one day? In the drawers of a maple chest in the dining room there are dusty porcelain teacups so thin they might crack the instant you lifted them to your lips.

We could steal everything in this house if we wanted and they probably wouldn't notice.

In the bathroom I pick up crystal and silver perfume bottles, a magnifying glass with a mother-of-pearl handle that rests atop a pile of ancient *Life* magazines. I pocket one of the perfume bottles, covering it with tissues taken from their nightstand.

On my way back, I hear Eddie laughing too loud and saying, "You're exactly right. You're a hundred percent on the mark."

Eddie gives them his card before we go, and he holds Mrs. Berner's hand in his. "If you decide you need a change, give Randall here a call. I think we can work a nice deal for all of us."

He turns to me. "I'll wait for you in the car," he says. He wants me to establish myself here. It will be my sale.

It will be easy. They're already leaning our way. They even like us, for God's sake. On my way out the door, I pull the perfume bottle out from the tissues and I hold it at my side, right there for them to see. Eddie's out in the car waiting. I stand in the doorway.

"Is there anything else I can answer for you?" I say.

She sees nothing.

"No," she says. "But I'm feeling sure there will be."

Eddie has me going it on my own so that he can move to other properties. In the last year, he's managed to buy two thousand acres of woodlands and waterfront in the Adirondacks, and our company has bought around seven times that. And these people really need the money from the looks of them. Ninety thousand dollars buys a new car, flat-screen TV, stereo and disc player, medicine and food for the next three years and a house on Collins Street, a block from the general store. Eddie's girlfriend says it's the Adirondacks. It's a special part of the country. And it is. Six million acres. Almost half of it unmarked, not even a logging road or snowmobile trail. The Hudson River starts up not too far from here in Lake Tear-of-the-Clouds. It's a lake almost a mile high, and I've been swimming there.

It's not as if we're building factories or a toxic waste dump. The houses and cabins we build are beautiful, state of the art: high ceilings, fireplaces, wraparound porches. And the outsides are left their natural wood color, or painted brown or grass green so they blend in with the earth. The way Eddie tells it, we're giving people their retirement and we are, but we're also making some coin. Like the Berners' three hundred acres. We'll split it into eight lots, each with a calendar picture of unspoiled Adirondack riverfront, and each selling for about four times what we'll pay the Berners. Our company places ads in the *New York Times* with pictures of the Oswegatchie, of the triple falls, the water dropping into spruce green eddies. "Five hours from the city and you're in God's backyard." People can't afford to buy beachfront anymore. They're sick of the suburbs, the shopping malls. We're giving them what they've been missing their whole lives. There's an interview process for the people who want to buy. "We want people who will respect the land," Eddie says, "who love the outdoors; people who will be good neighbors." I've never seen him turn down a buyer because he thought he'd be a bad neighbor. But people like to be interviewed. They want to think they've passed a test.

"Where'd you go?" he asks on the drive from the Berners'.

"I wasn't feeling that well."

"I think they're very interested. You need to get to know them. It's like I've been saying, low pressure. No one wants some salesman breathing down their neck. They don't trust that. Call them up in a few days just to talk. Don't ask her anything except how she's doing, the weather, Mr. Berner, and things like that and she'll invite you in for pie—I guarantee. And tell her about yourself a little. Ask her advice on something. I swear, it changes everything. Get them involved in your life a little. The sale has got to be secondary. You push too fast, like you were starting to in there, and people smell a rat."

We pass through rugged forest on our way into town.

"What kind of things do I tell her about myself?"

"Tell her about your family, about your mom and dad and how you worry about them from time to time. Tell her about visiting them. What that does is it makes you into a *son*. You're a salesman here, but you're also somebody's son. See what I'm saying?"

I am renting a three-room apartment directly above Latrell's General Store and across Collins Street from the post office. In the mornings I buy a cup of coffee and I sit in the back with the regulars, a bunch of old guys in baseball caps who smell like cigarettes. Vern Latrell knows me by my name now on most mornings, though once he called me Andy and another time Patrick. I corrected him both times because I want him to remember me. I want everyone around here to remember me because I will be here for a while. Eddie introduced me around my first week here. They all like Eddie. A couple of them have gone fishing with him. One old guy took him hunting. Eddie Callahan from Westchester County gumming around the woods hunting for deer. I tried to talk the way Eddie talked with them, loose and comfortable, one of the gang, but the words always came out wrong, stiff and unnatural, or else exaggerated, as though I were mimicking them. Now Eddie's moved away to meet another town full of homeowners, and he's left me behind as the new Eddie. No one has asked to take me hunting.

In a few days I call Mrs. Berner. She knows my voice before I identify myself.

"I was hoping you'd call, Randall," she says. "Have you gotten settled in yet?"

"All settled in at Eddie's old place. On top of Latrell's," I say. "Right there in the middle of town."

"You must be a little restless, huh?"

"What do you mean?"

"Not much for a young man like you to do around there, especially a young man whose roots are downstate."

"I like it. I'm getting to know everyone. All the regulars at Latrell's."

"That's a lazy bunch of do-nothings."

Weather, I think. "Days have been beautiful, huh? For October? I can't believe it. Is it always that beautiful?" Sunshine glazes my window.

"It's usually colder. But it's always beautiful."

"I think you're right," I say.

She says nothing. I say nothing. I can't think of anything else. She suspects me, I think. She knows about the perfume bottles. Good for her. Good for them. I'll say good-bye, I decide.

"Randall?" her voice creaks. "Do you like grilled cheese sandwiches with Virginia ham and tomato?"

"Yes," I say.

"Well, I do too. I would like you to come over to the house and have a sandwich with me."

Mr. Berner is in bed with the flu, she says. From time to time we hear a frightening cough from the other room. She brings him his sandwich. I wave from the doorway. He waves back pathetically. "Hello, Randall," he calls out. "Nice to see someone so young and healthy."

The rooms are so large I can't imagine how they heat the

place in the winter. I can imagine old Mr. Berner sick all winter in that cold house.

In the living room Mrs. Berner and I sit across from each other, me on the blue couch, her on the cloth-lined rocker.

"We've been discussing what you and Eddie brought up the other day. I'm starting to think it might make a whole world of sense."

Too fast, I think. Hold back. "But you've been here so long," I say. "It's got to be hard to think of moving from here."

"We'll go broke living here. And we don't get out that much to appreciate it that much anyhow."

I eat my sandwich. It is hot and gooey and as good as anything I can remember eating.

"I'm lonely all the time," she says. "You think you're teaching a lesson . . . "

She looks so sad I feel the need to cheer her up. "My mother and father are both retired. And they get such a kick out of my coming home," I say. "My mother makes a big deal out of it and she cooks some terrific meals. Sometimes my brothers come home at the same time. Family is important to me."

"What do your parents do?"

"Well, my father is a school custodian and my mother is a secretary in the military. She works for the army."

Neither of these are true. I haven't seen either of my parents in more than five years, and so I couldn't say precisely what they do. It doesn't seem like Mrs. Berner hears me anyhow.

"My mother just finished a tour in Kabul," I try.

"I wish you'd come by whenever you like and visit us, Randall," she says.

On the way back from the bathroom this time I take the

magnifying glass. I hold it at my side the way I did the perfume bottle as I say my good-byes. Mrs. Berner says nothing about it. She ducks back inside. On the way to my car I swipe the newspaper from the blue plastic box from the road.

That night I meet Eddie at a bar in Saranac Lake. He has two more prospective sellers lined up—another old couple, and a ninety-three-year-old widower. He's doing chores for the widower, bagging leaves and painting.

"I let him pay me a few dollars and a beer each time so he doesn't get suspicious or anything. I haven't even told him I work in real estate."

"What did you tell him?"

"I told him I was a social worker on sabbatical."

Eddie buys the beers and asks the bartender to make out a receipt. He knows the bartender's name and asks him about fishing on a particular section of the river.

"Caught two today," the bartender answers. "Walleyes have been hitting, Eddie. But it's just pan fish. Nothing too big."

"I can't even catch a cold lately," Eddie says.

It seems to me there are very few people Eddie doesn't know.

"What's new with the Berners?" he asks me when the bartender is out of earshot.

"Grilled cheese and Virginia ham today. Hamburgers and peach cobbler on Sunday night."

"Nice. *Nice.*"

"I'm following your advice. I'm taking it slow."

"Good, good. You're making a friend here. Not a sale. A *friend*. Remember that. You are helping them get to where they need to go. They can't survive in that place. When you're getting close, let me know and I'll write you out a check you can take over. She'll cry, I guarantee. She'll take one look at that ninety-thousand-dollar check and she'll cry."

I know that he's speaking the truth. In two or three meals, Mrs. Berner, Aurelia Berner, will do whatever I tell her because she trusts me and because she's lonely and wants to keep me as her friend or maybe as a fill-in for the kids who left for California. And I think that if it weren't me, it would certainly be someone else taking her money. And it isn't her money anyhow. It would be her money if she knew what her home was worth and she doesn't, so why should she make a fortune off a house and property she can't even use anymore?

Each time I visit the Berners I take something else, two of the snow globes, an old copy of *Robinson Crusoe,* a porcelain doll. I take three more perfume bottles. As we walk in the house I sometimes run my hand over the place where I took an object or two. I wonder where she keeps her cash, the money she probably pays a neighbor kid to do her grocery shopping.

I ask her once if she needs someone to do her grocery shopping.

I pick up a load of groceries for her and when I return with them I tell her they cost twice as much as they did. I want her to question me, to ask for a receipt. Instead she hands me fifty bucks for some cold cuts and fruit, bread, vegetables for a salad, and a few boxes of rice.

Old man Berner marks me some trails he hiked when he could walk and tells me what I'll see: "Thick red spruce and those nice fir trees in the highlands and lower down the sugar maples we get our syrup from, and beech and yellow birch, and animals, Randall, that you can't see anywhere else: Indian bats, grouses and loons, worm snakes and bog turtles, and turkey vultures." He reminds me a little of a turkey vulture, though I don't tell him that.

After a month or so, Eddie calls me in my room. "Did you get the check I sent?" he asks. My room looks like an antique shop. My place is filled with beautiful items taken from the Berners' house. I've dusted them all. I collected enough money from two things I sold to buy a secondhand TV and an electric razor. Soon I will have a great deal more than that. Eddie will pay me 3 percent of the profits, which could bring me about eight thousand dollars.

"They want out of there, Eddie. They're ready to sign whatever I bring over."

"Get her to sign and then give her the check. Make it fair. Ninety thousand just like we talked about. We're not in the business of ripping people off. We can't get that reputation."

It is clear he's convincing himself here and that he'd want to pay less. If he could get away with it, Eddie would buy their land for twenty-four dollars like the deal Peter Stuyvesant worked out for Manhattan.

The next weeks are freezing cold, the roads iced solid and scary to drive on. The winds whip harshly through whatever I put on. The snows come strong out of nowhere and I am forever scraping ice from my windows, knocking it out from under my boots. On my way home from the Berners' one night I am stuck in a whiteout, white all around me, and I cannot tell which direction is forward. There aren't any sounds. My tires are high off the road in a snow cloud. I slow to about five miles an hour and then I cut the engine. I step out of the car and let the snow fall on me and for just a moment I feel like a six-year-old.

When I get back in and start driving again, it takes me two hours to go a distance that should take twenty minutes.

At night I watch TV just to hear the voices. I take long walks and then I turn on the news. There's a small mention of the man who killed the old couple in Utica. He claims he never meant to kill them. He meant to rob them but the old guy pulled out a knife. The reporter said the knife was the old man's Swiss Army knife and the blade was smaller than four inches.

On the night of a particularly loud and icy storm, I barricade myself in blankets against the sounds outside. I wear layers of sweaters and shirts. Before I go to sleep my phone rings.

"Randall?"

It's Mrs. Berner.

"There are two windows I can't get closed. They're wide open and the heat's going right through them. I'm afraid he'll . . . I'm afraid Mr. Berner will freeze if we don't get the windows closed."

They are hard to close even for me. I pull and pull and then I begin banging on them. I pour steaming water in the openings and then smear butter in the hinges. The cold air washes in against my face. Finally one budges and in another few minutes I've got the other closed.

Mrs. Berner gasps. And then she gives me a beautiful smile. We sit in her kitchen and drink hot chocolate, and the sound of old Roury Berner snoring, loud and steady, comforts us both, like the sound of the logs crackling in the wood-burning stove.

Sunday the sun comes out strong. The ground begins to thaw. I eat turkey at the Berners'. Mr. Berner eats a few bites of dinner with us and then heads back to bed.

"I guess we've been pressing our good luck," Mrs. Berner says. "He's getting worse living here. He's going downhill."

After dinner I bring out the papers. Mrs. Berner looks them over closely. She shuts me out for a while and I think for a moment she might lose her nerve and decide to stay. But then she looks up at me and smiles.

"You might want to think about this awhile."

"I have," she says. "Where do I sign?"

I show her.

"Now I give you this check for ninety thousand. You fill out a check for two thousand and make it out to me. That's a transaction fee."

"Transaction fee. Okay."

"That leaves you with eighty-eight thousand."

"That's plenty."

And then we have nothing to say to each other. I drink my hot chocolate and she drinks hers.

Half an hour later I pull my coat on to leave.

"Randall," she says before I'm out the door.

"Yes," I say.

"We want you to have those things. I wanted you to know that."

"What?"

"The things you've been taking. We want you to enjoy them."

I feel dizzy suddenly. I can hear Mr. Berner coughing.

"You're welcome to have anything of ours you want. We don't have anyone to give things to anymore. You know what that's like?"

"Thank you," I say.

"I picture our things in your little apartment over the general store. I picture you taking them into your home when you buy one. You'll have a nice home, one day. Maybe you'll choose to stay around here. We'd like you to. We'd like you to think of us as your family."

"Thank you," I say. I tell her I'll help her move.

"You're not who you think you are," she says before I can get away. "Give it time. I know. You'll find your peace."

The door is open, but I stand still and seen before her, unable to move, overcome with a feeling I cannot name—the sense of being followed.

"You think you're stealing, but it's *yours*, don't you see? Always was. You're *forgiven*, Randall. Money shouldn't divide. The past is over and done."

It's clear from her eyes she's talking about someone else, someone she blames herself for losing years ago, but I pretend she's talking to me.

"We love you very much," she says.

"I know that," I say.

HOW TO FALL

I *rode up to the snow-blessed hills* of Vermont on a ski trip for singles. I did. Two overheated buses full of women and men between the ages of twenty-two and thirty drinking flavored vodka from plastic martini glasses, and trying to mask their awkwardness. My college roommate, Amanda, dragged me along, in part for company, but mostly to extract me from the ditch I'd dropped into since things ended with Mitchell. I was permitted to mention Mitchell once—for under ten minutes—Amanda said. The subject was otherwise off-limits.

"Deal," I said.

"Let's see," Amanda said.

There were a few more women on the trip than men, not by design, but two of the men had called in sick at the last moment and another—the one I decided I would have hooked up with— was in Florida arranging his grandfather's funeral.

A broadsheet was circulating with miniprofiles of all of us, and pictures of everyone but me (I'd signed on too late). Amanda quickly sized up the talent—dentist, doctor, actor, shrink . . . software engineer, sports agent, magazine editor . . . and she picked out two lawyers, Kevin and Roland, who worked for the same public interest firm and were sitting two rows back from us. Kevin's hair was thinning and his gray eyes were slightly amused. Roland, who wore a pale blue ski cap, had a wide smile, the patchy beginnings of a beard, and attractive lines around his mouth. They seemed charming enough in our initial conversation, and if I pretended I was someone else, I could get through this, I thought.

We were booked into a fairly large bed-and-breakfast—eight rooms, and Amanda arranged it so our room was next to the lawyers. It was around nine when we arrived. Killington, Vermont. We went straight out for dinner. There were other singles at our table, all perfectly harmless, but after they cleared the salads, we confined our conversation to the four of us. The lawyers were telling stories of spectacular ski accidents from their childhoods. Roland used to race. He'd had a nearly fatal collision with a tree when he was seventeen and lay in a coma for a week. They were certain he would die or end up a vegetable. "I think my brother had already made plans to move into my room."

He closed and opened his eyes as though reenacting it for us.

"Then one day I just woke up."

"He transmogrified," Kevin said.

We waited for an explanation.

For around half a year—while he convalesced from his broken leg and two broken ribs—all the murkiness and "fuckedupness" in his adolescent life disappeared, he said. His grades improved. He wrote a play (loosely based on his hospital stay) that earned him raves in the school newspaper, and he learned how to play the French horn. He read *War and Peace*.

"It was as though I'd cleared out all the clutter in my brain and I suddenly had room for everything I'd wanted to do. It lasted until the summer after graduation."

Kevin refilled everyone's wineglasses. We looked at Roland now, who seemed uncomfortable with the attention he'd drawn.

"Then I went back to ripping off convenience stores," he said. I believed him until the corner of his mouth turned up in a smile.

"He was a God as a racer," Kevin said.

"I'm far more restrained these days," he said.

"His restraint would make your hair stand on end," Kevin said. "I'm Mister Leisure out there. I snowboard with the high-school dudes."

"How old are you?" Amanda asked him.

"Thirty."

"Have you ever been married?"

Amanda was a financial analyst and accustomed to gathering information before committing her clients' resources. I shot her a look.

"Yes," he said.

"Somehow I knew it," Amanda said.

"She died," Kevin said. "Not from skiing."

"I'm so sorry. How did she die?" Amanda asked.

"She had an aneurysm," he said. "Listen, I don't want to depress everyone. It was a while ago."

"Two years," Roland said.

"You poor, poor thing." Amanda leaned toward Kevin with increased interest. "My uncle had cancer. He's better now. They got to him early, I guess. How old was she?"

"Twenty-six."

"My God, that's so *young*."

"It is." He fidgeted with the clasp on his leather watchband. "Anyway, how long have you guys lived in the city?"

"My whole life," I said.

"Five years," Amanda said, about herself. Then she told them about my childhood. It was a sweet gesture, I suppose, though she mangled several details and made me sound fairly disturbed (and my father sound like a polygamist). While she was talking, I started to picture Kevin's young wife a day before her death, booking a vacation she'd never take, or buying groceries she'd never eat, and then I remembered Mitchell and I realized he was at a secure distance now, and I felt calm, because when you got right down to it, what had happened to me? Nothing life-threatening. No coma, no aneurysm.

I poured myself another glass of wine. Then two more, and we had shots of vodka after that, which Amanda said should be our last.

We started telling jokes. Or maybe I just did. I told them the one about the city boy moving upstate. He gets invited to a party by his downstairs neighbor.

"What'll it be like?"

"Oh, it's going to be wild," the guy says. "There's going to be some *drinking*, there's gonna be some fuckin'; they'll be some fightin', and maybe a little dancin'."

"Who all's coming?" the city boy asks.

"Oh, it's just going to be you and me."

I'm not sure why I told that one, or why I thought it was so funny. But the men laughed and Amanda didn't.

"So the first guy gets raped," she said.

"No," I said. "That's not it at all."

"So then what is it?"

"It's about false advertising," I said.

Roland raised his glass. "And that underneath it all we just want to drink, fuck, fight, and dance."

The night he broke up with me, Mitchell and I decided to sleep together one final time, and when he slipped out the front door in the morning, I felt surprisingly intact. I had the typical what-did-you-do-over-the-weekend conversations at the media distribution company where I work, accomplished a few basic tasks, and I thought, *Maybe this'll be easy.* And then I thought, *What does it mean if it's easy?* And then I started to call Mitchell to ask him what it meant. But I remembered the rule we made about not calling and so I hung up.

I went after work to the Museum of Natural History, and I coursed around my favorite spots, the whale and the dinosaurs, and the Pygmies. I tried to make it fun, so that it would be a story I'd tell my friends—*You know what I did? I went to a museum by myself and you know what? I had a blast.* And they'd think—She's going to be just fine. I've always liked seeing people alone in museums, jotting down notes, lingering at a painting or a piece of Mayan pottery. I liked the idea that I could be like that. But I began to feel very self-conscious, and I wanted to get to a phone so I could call Mitchell. I had left my cell phone at home so I wouldn't be tempted.

* * *

I hightailed it through the park. It was November and fairly cold, and you could see smoke emerging from the mouths of the bundled-up joggers and shoppers who passed by. I began to think that going out without a phone had been a mistake. I wondered, *What if he calls?*

He called, I thought. Or stopped by to make up and I wasn't there. Convinced that this would happen, I stayed in the next few nights watching DVDs. I chose ones I thought would distract me, like *The Matrix*, which with my diminished concentration I couldn't really follow—people in pods, and a world that might or might not exist, and Keanu Reeves in a black coat taking pills and shooting people up in what looked like the entrance to a bank.

At eleven the following Sunday night, I called Mitchell and told him that if he came over and we slept together it didn't have to mean anything.

Brilliant move.

It was two weeks before I heard from him. And over those nights it was like I imagine life must be in a methadone clinic—cold sweats and a soul-shriveling restlessness—but this is nothing new. Everyone in every country of the world has bushwhacked through this. It probably didn't help that we slept together twice more. I have no explanation other than that both times I believed we were back together, though he explicitly told me ("Are we *clear* on this, Jen?") we weren't. When I left at three and searched for a cab, I did this thing where I dug my fingernails, and one time a pencil, into my arms, the way I would as a little girl when the doctor gave me a shot and I wanted to divert the pain. I saw my reflection once in the wide-angle mirror of my apartment building's lobby. My hair was squashed and matted and my arms were blotched with little red cuts. I looked like a junkie with shitty aim.

Under the silky light of a storybook moon, the four of us walked back through the cold to the B and B. The proprietress was at her desk when we arrived and she asked us for our breakfast preferences. She handed us sheets of pale green paper with an impressive list of food and beverage selections. I circled grapefruit juice and pancakes, and bacon, and then thought better of it and crossed out the bacon, and then wrote out the word *bacon*, and then wrote the word *Yes* next to bacon, so they would know I wanted it. What the fuck. I asked for a pot of coffee—it said a cup or a pot, and I liked the idea of someone brewing a whole pot just for me.

We turned in our lists and then we lingered in front of our room. A dog barked from downstairs. I thought Amanda might ask the men in and I would have gone along with it, but it was better we went our separate ways. The rooms were small and one of us might have felt trapped. We could hear their voices through the walls though we couldn't make out what they were saying, even when we listened through the water glasses.

At the mountain the next morning I was the lone member of our foursome who had to rent equipment. In the rental shop I began to feel jittery. I was a car ride away from my phone. I saw a couple getting their skis fitted, and it occurred to me that Mitchell might have a new girlfriend by now. And then I thought, *What if they're here?* Or *What if I run into them?*

When I returned outside, Roland was waiting for me. He said Kevin and Amanda hadn't wanted to wait but that they'd meet up with us at lunch.

"You'll be bored to tears," I said.

"I won't in the slightest," he said, and then I remembered this was a *singles* trip. It now felt awkward, the idea of skiing all morning with Roland the racer, who'd start guiding me through my intermediate turns like I was twelve. But there was no other choice really, so I decided to make the best of it.

We began one of those personal résumé conversations, and for the first trip up it went well enough. But on the second ride I drew back, like I was spoken for, which, of course, was absurd. I encouraged him to tell more stories of ski accidents he'd witnessed or heard about. By our third run I was convinced I would die on the mountain—that I would hit a tree, or land on a jagged rock formation, or fall a few thousand yards head over heels until my lifeless body came to rest in a pile of white.

I fell five times before lunch, twice face-first because I'd crossed my tips, and in each instant Roland was there to carry my lost ski to me and say encouraging things like, "You were really *feeling* it there."

I couldn't have been much fun, as I drifted more than once on our chairlift rides into a private theater wherein I was screening a movie of me and Mitchell in Cape May, when we stared at the sky until five and then slept together in our bathing suits on a lounge chair on our hotel room deck, next to a pitcher of daiquiris. We barely moved the whole day and in those hot dreamy hours something in me altered. Mitchell slipped out that evening and didn't come back for two hours. I remember heading out in my bare feet searching for him down side streets and through shop windows. I had a panic attack, sweats and heart palpitations, until I saw him again two blocks from the hotel in his tight black T-shirt and jeans, carrying two clear plastic boxes with steaks and mashed potatoes from a restaurant. He was perplexed by the sight of me out on the sidewalk, with no shoes, in just a T-shirt and my bikini bottom.

"Where were you going?" he asked.

"I thought you weren't coming back."

He stared in disbelief.

"Do you have any idea how twisted that is?" he said.

Toward the top of the lift we saw Amanda and Kevin on the slope below us. Roland yelled out, "Yo, *Devil Dog!*" and Kevin looked up. I decided to yell "Yo, *DeManding!*" but Amanda kept carefully carving out her Jacqueline Kennedy turns, for our benefit. Roland pointed to his watch, which meant we'd meet in the lodge. Kevin nodded and then flew across the hill, with his arms gracefully spread out like some sort of snowboarding angel.

That night we planned to hit the heated pool and Jacuzzi at a newly remodeled resort. All the single young professionals would be there and there were supposed to be drinks and a DJ. Amanda, who spent an hour every afternoon at the gym working on her quads and glutes, was excited. I really didn't feel like getting into a pool with strangers and drinking, and hanging about in a bikini.

I checked my cell phone when I got back: another message

from my mother and one from 24-Hour Fitness asking me if I'd dropped my membership.

Amanda was upset that I was going to miss the pool party and she said it would throw off the chemistry of the whole weekend. And wasn't I interested in Roland?

"He's about a billion times smarter and handsomer than *what's-his-name.*"

She said she really liked this guy Kevin. They'd talked the whole day about his wife's death, and they'd broken through some barriers. She said he was a pretty remarkable and resilient guy. And I thought there was something pathetic and even ghoulish about using a conversation about a man's dead wife's brain aneurysm as a way to get him to like her, though I stayed silent because over the years I'd used my own methods to get people to like me.

I said I was getting dinner alone, and that I might watch a pay-per-view movie on television.

"There are no pay-per-view movies," she said testily. "It isn't a Holiday Inn."

"Then I'll read," I said.

"That sounds really fun."

"If it isn't, I'll know where to find you."

"Oh, come do this with us, Jen. It's going to be such a blast. It'll be *good* for you. You're not going to have a lot of chances like this."

I nearly said something very unkind to Amanda, but I knew she just wanted us to be better friends and that I was letting her down.

"Maybe I'll come by later," I said.

* * *

I went out to a nearby restaurant by myself and ate a bad Cajun
chicken sandwich and a Caesar salad with around a half gallon of
dressing on it. The TV that hung over the bar played sports, college basketball from some place in the Midwest. Lots of corn-fed
white boys. The waiter asked me where I was from and I lied and
told him "the Hawaiian Islands." I have no idea why I said that.
And why not Hawaii? Why *the Hawaiian Islands?* He told another
waiter who came by and said he was planning his honeymoon and
wanted to know where in Hawaii to go. The Big Island, I said, because I'd heard it was the nicest and he seemed nice and I wanted
to give him the best information I had. I tipped my waiter twenty
dollars because I'd lied to him. At this rate I was likely to be broke
by the time I got to lunch the next day.

I thought about heading over to the party at the hot pool. I
really did. And maybe it would have been fun but I kept running
the wrong film in my mind, of us all in the water, Amanda on
someone's shoulders trying to pull another woman off some guy.
And me feeling tired, and unhappy, and fat, and wet.

The TV didn't really work. And reading felt too lonely. The
longer the night went on, the more I dreaded skiing again with
Roland, and the more I thought it was likely he'd take me on a
run beyond my ability. It had turned much colder since it rained
earlier in the evening and I knew that meant ice. The whole
thing felt wrong to me anyway—Amanda and her widower;
Roland the ski instructor, sweet as he was, and so dauntingly
beautiful on the slopes, either getting me killed, or following
after me all day long like a doting dad. I could insist on skiing
alone, but that would be the most depressing, I thought, and so
I decided to leave.

* * *

I wrote a note to Amanda and told her to apologize to the men, and to the trip organizers—I could hear her lecture—*These trips are important to me,* and *Everything was going so well. When are you going to start acting like a member of the human race,* or whatever.

I didn't have a ride, so I took a taxi to the bus station. There was a nine o'clock bus that would get me in at 4:30 in the morning.

Odd choice to be making, I suppose.

I bought the ticket, and I got onto the bus. A couple of other skiers followed, but mostly the bus was empty, and it smelled like spilled beer. A man in a camouflage army jacket was sleeping in the front seat, and a mother and daughter were holding a very intense conversation in the middle of the bus. I sat in the back. I had two books with me, but I was far too distracted to read. I tried to go to sleep but mostly I just stared out of the window feeling sorry for myself and making new blotches on my arms. At one point I said loudly, "Get *the fuck* over it," and the mother turned around, and glared at me.

"What the hell do you know?" she said.

I made it to my apartment without further incident at 5:15 A.M. There were no messages on either the home phone or my cell, which I'd turned off, and then on, and then off again, all night.

I slept until two. I had terrible dreams. Keanu Reeves was in one. He was standing atop a cliff and held his arm out to save me, and instead I pulled him down and we both went tumbling until we dropped into a freezing lake.

When I checked my cell, there was a message from Amanda. Her tone had the crisp exasperation of someone lodging a complaint with an airline. I had left my skis and boots in the closet—and she was going to have to return them and retrieve my credit card.

A week went by and then the new intern at work told me there was a man on the phone asking for me. It was Roland, calling to check in. Hearing his voice made me feel happy. I apologized for leaving the ski trip so abruptly, and he said, "You can make amends by going to dinner with me."

I surprised myself by saying that I'd like that.

That Friday we went to dinner at a Peruvian place in the Village. I barely recognized him outside the entrance to the restaurant. He had on a woolen blazer over a black, collared shirt. His hair was thick and brushed back from his face, which was clean-shaven. He started to apologize for his accident stories and I wouldn't let him. I wanted to talk about other things.

He walked me all the way uptown to my apartment building afterward and hugged me good night. He might have been hoping for more, or maybe I was. I felt like a different and improved person, at the awkward end of a good first date.

"I'm sorry I got into all that at dinner," I said. I told him a little about Mitchell. Maybe more than a little.

"Don't sweat it," he said. He said it was normal to go through what I was going through, that he read once that an abandoned rhesus monkey will sleep sporadically, drink sparsely, and lose all interest in food.

"Their immune system breaks down," he said. "They get sick easily; and they die in great numbers."

"I bet you use that line on all the girls," I said.

"Only the bookish ones," he said.

In the middle of the night I grabbed the phone and hit redial, because I'd tried to call Mitchell after work; but I must have called Roland's number after that because he answered. I was pretty out of it and I said, "Can you *please* come over?" believing it was Mitchell, and Roland said, "I'll be there in twenty minutes."

When he came over, I said something very stupid. I said maybe I'd become a better person if I fell in and out of a coma the way he had.

"It's never that black-and-white," he said, and gave me a test-smile to see if I'd been kidding.

I asked him about when he was out, what that was like.

"It was like dying . . . and dreaming at the same time— there are specific things I remember about it, the shape of a sound; time skipping backward and forward. A conversation about blood types."

"What sort of things did you learn?"

"*Learn?* Hmmm. That I would die someday. That I had wasted a lot of time worrying about things that weren't important. It sounds trite when you say this sort of stuff aloud. It's a bit like in chess, when you can see the next three moves? I could do that. I could see the traps."

"Do you want to sleep over?"

"I do," he said. "But not tonight. How about tomorrow night?"

He was playing this perfectly.

* * *

He came over the next night with five different boxes of Chinese food, a six-pack of Tsingtao, and a movie. I ate a little of everything and drank two and a half beers. My fortune cookie said that I was comfortable in my own skin, which didn't really sound like a fortune, and certainly not mine. "They should call them compliment cookies," Roland said. His fortune said that he was wise in the way of finances. We imagined disparaging fortunes we'd sneak into Chinese restaurants. "Your spouse will be unfaithful and your children will dislike you," I said, reading mine.

"Your investments will tank and the bank will seize your home," he said.

I watched him as we polished off our beers and I could see this turning into something. I laughed out loud for no reason, a goofy, raucous sound that shocked me. He kissed me then and I kissed him back. And then we were rolling around on the floor, groping for body parts and kissing necks and shoulders. He had a much more athletic body than Mitchell, who, when you got right down to it, was too tall and too thin, his voice too raspy from cigarettes, his hair too long and directionless, until he cruelly buzzed it short (the way I'd urged him to have it cut) the week *after* we broke up. We started pulling at each other's clothes, and somewhere along the way I fell off the ride and back into the ditch.

Roland beamed at me affectionately, and I felt suffocated.

"I like this," he said.

"Me too," I said, slithering out from beneath him. "Let's go get some air."

* * *

There was a soft snowfall outside and we decided to go sledding in the park. We passed Tavern on the Green with its garish holiday lights, and the honeyed words of a torch song streaming through an opened window; then we walked by Sheep Meadow and the Bandshell, uptown until we found the park's hidden sledding spots. Mitchell had found two long planks of cardboard in the recycling bins of my building, and we used them as sleds. Did I say Mitchell? *Roland.* We climbed to the top of the hill—Dog Hill, they call it, or more precisely Dog Shit Hill, because a lot of dogs do just that, only it's hidden way beneath the snow. It was very cold, and the ground felt hard, even as the new snow was falling. The sledding would be fast. I got a running start and jumped on the cardboard and I yelled out at the top of my lungs, "*Shit be gone!*" Which felt good, and liberating.

Roland followed me yelling the same thing, even louder. The cardboard glided nicely over the crunchy snow. The ground whipped by, and I could feel every bump and hard-cornered chunk of ice. I laid my body luge-style, and then I soared off of a sudden rise and flipped into the air for a full second and a half. The ground smacked my head, and for a moment it knocked me out, as though I'd inhaled the gas from a whipping cream canister, like we did in high school. I saw a trail of light like a comet in the sky, and then the world spun around me, white and dazzling. I gathered myself to my feet and went running back up the hill. Roland was already there. We started up again, faster this time. "This is completely crazy," he said, with a reasonable, kind smile that I wanted to love. I wanted this. I allowed myself to believe it was possible. I could crash into a tree, or a rock, or a bank of snow, and land hard enough so that something inside me would break. I would stay out here, burning down the steep dark hill until it happened.

LETTERS FROM THE ACADEMY

Dear Mr. Wilcox,

I would like to let you know how your son Lee is progressing at the Tennis Academy. I've chosen to communicate by letter because I believe what we're witnessing requires more than a casual phone call or email, as I suspect you will agree.

I should start by confessing that I did not at the outset peg Lee as a star player. Your son was a bit spacey, and antisocial really, whereas the main cadre of top players cling to one another like a pack of young wolves. Lee has a tendency to look away when you speak so that it appears he isn't listening, though it has been my experience, as I'm sure it has been yours, that he's heard every word. He has invariably incorporated what I've suggested into his game.

But by the second week I'd see him staying late in front of the backboard and hitting way into the night, and there again at dawn with a hopper of balls and the targets, practicing a thousand or more serves. And now, a month in, I can see just a little Becker

in his volleys and a touch of Agassi in his returns. I do not use
those terms lightly. In the last tournament Lee was made to play
the fourth seed, a boy from Kentucky with a huge serve-and-volley
game, and Lee destroyed him in straight sets—6–2, 6–2. He never
brags about his accomplishments, but I figured Lee would have
told you this; when I talked to him a few days afterward, though,
I understood that he probably didn't. He said he hasn't spoken to
you in a while.

Lee won two other matches in that tournament, and when
he finally lost, it was because of a broken string that forced him
to borrow a racket. I plan to make a deal with Wilson so that
Lee can begin to receive free equipment. I hope this will be
an arrangement you will go along with. There is nothing you
would need to do financially, but Lee would have to wear only
Wilson clothes and use only Wilson rackets. In all other respects,
I now think, he is ready for the responsibility such a deal would
entail.

He still reads all the time when he isn't practicing and I
wonder if that's what's caused his eyes to deteriorate. Usually he
wears his contacts when he's playing but sometimes he wears
those thick glasses, which makes other kids poke fun at him,
although to his credit he doesn't seem to listen to them or care all
that much. I'm not sure if he has any real friends here, other than
a boy from the school our athletes attend who doesn't play tennis,
but who watches Lee play. This boy smokes cigarettes, which
I certainly hope Lee does not do, because it would result in his
suspension from the Academy. So far, so good. There have been
no issues with girls, although a few seem to be taking interest in
him. I don't think it would be all that bad for Lee to go on a date
or two, but I have not spoken to him about it, and I imagine that's

more your territory than mine. There have been off-color things said about Lee and the boy from the school, although that's what's always said about unusual kids. I have caught Lee staring a few times at Vivi, the girl from Denmark, who is one of our best players and is something to look at.

What is so remarkable about Lee is his ability to focus on a single task, so unusual for a boy his age, or for anyone at any age. The world recedes for Lee when he is on the court, and his face looks purposefully placid, like Borg's or Lendl's. It's rather intimidating, really. And he has a terrific sense of balance. As he runs, you can imagine him keeping a stack of books over his head and not spilling one. His racket speed has improved, as has his footwork. These improvements are incremental, and barely detectable day to day, but I'm beginning to think he'll be one of our top players by this spring. It will be a different life for him, and perhaps for you, because I believe he will be traveling soon for tournaments, perhaps to the nationals. And I for one would like to be part of that.

I think that tennis isn't really all that important to Lee, but that whatever is in front of him becomes important, and tennis has been in front of him. He has a remarkable memory and seems to be able to read a book a night. I'm not sure I've ever seen him particularly upset, or all that happy, although when he's hanging out with the boy who smokes cigarettes and when he's watching Vivi play, he becomes more animated. That is all I can tell you right now. I hope this is as exciting to you as it is to us at the Academy. We are expecting very big things from Lee.

Sincerely yours,

Maximilian Gross

My Dear Mr. Wilcox,

    I fear you have been out of town and therefore unable
to reply to my last letter, or else you've read it and may still
respond. I wanted to fill you in on the progress since our last
correspondence, if we can call it progress, and I think we can.
Lee has been practicing even harder, sharpening his footwork
and volleying. It has gotten so that five boys can strike shots
at him nearly simultaneously and he will cleanly volley all five
balls back. He can retrieve the deepest lob after nearly touching
the net, then sprint back for a drop shot on the opposite side of
the court. The player who comes to mind when he does this is
Wilander, or maybe Borg, whose fitness was legendary. Wilson
has sent the first shipment of rackets, and I have strung them
each with a combination of gut and synthetic nylon at fifty-two
pounds, which allows for a tremendous amount of topspin but
means that on flat shots Lee will still be able to keep the ball
in the court. The boy he hangs out with has lately taken to
smoking a pipe and wearing an army cap. Lee's grades have been
outstanding in all his classes except for public speaking, where he
got a B-. At sixteen, he reads at the graduate-school level, and his
vocabulary is that of a man twice his age.

    I have signed Lee up for a series of satellite tournaments,
which will bring him in front of some significant crowds and
provide us with a good testing ground. I very rarely tell a parent
that their son or daughter has what it takes to make a living at
our sport, but in Lee's case it is becoming apparent to us all. Just
last week a collegiate player from Florida Tech stopped by the
Academy to train with Lee. At the end of the day they played a set
and Lee thrashed him 6–1. It was only practice and the collegiate
player, one of our alums, was somewhat out of shape, due to a
monthlong spell of mononucleosis. But the margin of victory was

what sent shock waves that night through the Academy dining room.

I am concerned because we have not received your check for the spring, and while I'm quite confident that Lee will qualify for a full scholarship, I would like to talk to you about this and other matters, preferably on the telephone so there can be some back-and-forth. It would be better still if you could make the trip down here and see what your son's life is like. The other day I observed Lee and the Danish girl sitting on the practice court bench after a long workout, the two of them quite sweaty and flush, and I saw the Danish girl several times touching Lee's arm, and then resting her head on his shoulder. Again, I cannot be sure if there was anything significant going on, and nor would it be a problem, as the Danish girl is from a good family and is an extremely talented player ranked very high in Denmark. I only think that Lee would profit from some adult guidance on this matter.

The boy who smokes cigarettes is also a friend of the Danish girl. I saw him out on the court one night in blue jeans and the wrong shoes hitting balls with Lee while the Danish girl watched. We have strict dress rules at the Academy, and strict rules about allowing guests to play without clearing them through Clara at the front desk. I spoke to Lee about this and he assured me the smoker would not be playing at the Academy again. The three of them ate together at a table at the side of the pool, pizza slices cribbed from the Academy pizza party. I did not see this as a problem and would like Lee to feel he has freedom here and isn't being watched around the clock. There are entire days in which I barely see Lee, though not an hour passes without my thinking of something else we might do to optimize his prodigious talent.

There is a junior Davis Cup player coming to the Academy from Chile, a boy whose game harkens back to a young Yannick Noah, and I would like to have Lee play him in a match inside the newly refurbished Academy stadium. The match will be videotaped, and we will post clips of the most exciting points on the Academy website provided it goes well and Lee is successful, as I'm quite certain he will be.

    With warm regards and in distant partnership,
    Maximilian Gross

Dear Mr. Wilcox,

    The match with Javier, the Chilean junior, was more than my middle-aged heart could take. In the warm-ups Lee was relaxed, powdering his ground strokes and crushing his overheads, and he took a 5–1 lead in the first set. But after that he began to spray shots, and double-fault, like a pitcher who mysteriously and suddenly loses control. I have seen this sort of meltdown eight or nine times, but it usually occurs for boys with more volatile temperaments than Lee's. It might have served as a lesson had Lee in fact lost the match, but Javier had his own, more theatrical and subequatorial meltdown in the third set, and Lee won through attrition more than perseverance.

    When the match was over, Lee and the boy who smokes went to the movie theater at the mall. I saw them buy two pretzels, a slushy, and a chicken sandwich of suspect pedigree. They sat in the eighth row. I know this because I was in the fifteenth. It is not unusual for me to go to the movies, and I hadn't intended to spy on them, but the movie was at a convenient time for me, and I planned to leave before the end of the film so as not to inhibit them on their afternoon escape. There are no rules against seeing a movie on a Sunday, provided you make it back by dinnertime, and provided you've played at least four hours and run three miles, which Lee had done. I heard Lee laugh several times during the movie, once at a very serious, and in fact poignant, moment—a last conversation in a hospital ward between a husband and wife—and I'm quite sure he and the smoker were upsetting the family who sat in front of them.

The other boys at the Academy had a basketball tournament that night to which Lee declined participation and instead played cards with one of the groundskeepers in the groundskeeper shack. Money was involved and Lee apparently ended up on the short end. I don't think it was a disastrous defeat, perhaps $100, but I suspect that Lee has been paying the groundskeeper back with some of the Wilson equipment he has been receiving. The basketball game went on until after ten, and afterward the boys drank Gatorade together on the Academy porch. Lee was back in his room by then, reading or doing sit-ups. (I have tried to match him in his exercise routine and am up to 125 sit-ups and 100 push-ups a day, which is not bad I would say for a man of forty-four.) Thank you for the quick note you sent, which I know was written during a particularly busy time for you. And in answer to your question, yes, there are several other coaches who work directly with Lee, and he is not being singled out for special treatment. But I must say that if he was, it would be because he is not an ordinary adolescent, and not an ordinary talent.

I am considering banning the smoking boy from the Academy grounds, but am reluctant to do so because I fear Lee would flee like a hostage from a barricaded embassy. Mostly my time is spent scheduling more matches for Lee and better practice partners. This weekend we will go to Boca Raton for a tournament at the Escondido Club. They have not seeded Lee and have no idea what they are about to see. I know that wherever Mrs. Wilcox is, and I choose not to believe the rumors, she is beaming with pride right now, as you in your own way must be. Lately in his forehand I am seeing a little of Jim Courier in the two years he won the French, and in his footwork I have noticed an aspect of Gustavo Kuerten. I believe too that the Danish girl is now in love with Lee, as I saw her leaving a note outside his door the other night. I admit I did lift the note and thought of opening it, but did not. I relate this to you to indicate that I do not want to get in the way of Lee and his friendships. I will write to you from the Escondido Club, undoubtedly with exciting news. There is a rumor that Sampras might stop in to watch a match or two. Wouldn't that be something?

Yours,

Maximilian Gross

Dearest Mr. Wilcox,

I am writing you from the veranda at the Escondido, which is filled with players and parents and coaches, much of South Florida's tennis aristocracy. Lee is one of four Academy players entered in the tournament, and from where I sit I can see him rallying with a junior player from Taiwan.

I'm happy to report that Pete Sampras is indeed staying at the Escondido and was seen this morning at the breakfast buffet with his movie-star wife and their two sons. It is hard to see Sampras eating his eggs and oatmeal and sausages and not think of how many times on the brink of a Grand Slam he flamed out so impotently in the French. There is nothing sadder than seeing a big hitter stumble and struggle on slow clay.

I wonder how much of you is in Lee, and whether in your

early days with the All-City Orchestra and later with Stan Kenton
and Lionel Hampton you were equally intense and abstracted. I
must say that I've always loved your work. Lee told me yesterday
about the first time he saw you perform, when he was eleven and
you were in Montreal. I now own a dozen of your CDs and I play
them in the morning when I awake and drink my coffee.

In the evenings Lee goes boogie boarding with Vivi, which
I think is perfectly healthy, though I know some coaches might
discourage such activities. In Lee's case I think we should
welcome any broadening of his interests—moments in which he
can be a kid, if you will.

As for our reason for being here, Lee did as well as we could
have hoped. We played him up an age group, in the 18s, and he
won his first three matches before losing to the second seed.
Sampras watched four or five games of Lee's defeat and said—
these are his exact words—"This kid is pretty good." I wish you
could have been there to hear this, but I hope you can imagine
yourself where I was, hearing such a career-making compliment!

I was thinking of you, Mr. Wilcox, and what you might
have done in this instance, how you would have responded. I was
channeling the moment in the Frankfurt documentary where you
take that pretentious journalist to task.

"You bet your fucking ass," he is, I said, though it is far from
my nature to use that sort of language, and certainly not in front
of the greatest champion in our sport. I may have said some other
things to the hotel staff there, who warned me to be quiet. I was
escorted to my room and asked to leave first thing in the morning.

The fuck I will, I thought.

I watched the end of Lee's match from my room. I thought
the last match might go on forever. Do you know those rallies
where each of you digs to the bottom and reaches his racket out

and manages the strength to knock the ball across again, and then sprints on strained calves and cramping stomach back to the center of the court for more? Was it like that on those late nights when you played one last set at Birdland?

From where does genius arise?

When he lost, Lee shook the other boy's hand and then went down to the beach and watched the ocean for an hour or so. I joined him there and took him to one of the restaurants inside where I bought him a fish dinner, which he ate without a word.

"Would it be okay if I stopped playing for a while?" he asked me afterward.

"Why would you stop playing?"

"I feel tired," he said.

"Are we talking a few days? A week?"

"I don't know," he said. "Maybe more than a week."

"Whatever you need," I said. And then he collapsed.

There was a doctor in the hotel who said it was simply heat exhaustion and cramps. They told him to rest with a cold washcloth on his forehead, and to drink electrolytes. At around eleven he went downstairs with the Danish girl. They sat by the pool with their feet in the water. I watched them for a while and then went to bed.

In the morning Lee was on the court, hitting with Pete Sampras as though none of this had happened. I stood on the veranda with my suitcase packed, waiting for a taxi to come and take me to another hotel. Sampras kept staring over at me, unsmiling. May I say here that the champ has not aged terribly well? Not in his face anyhow. The sun has been particularly unkind to him, giving him the deep lines of an aging lifeguard. Nor has his hairline held up as he must have hoped.

When they'd concluded their workout, Sampras told me I

should stay away from Lee and that Lee would be traveling with Pete as his practice partner.

My face felt hot, and my jaw tightened.

"But you don't play tournaments anymore," I said.

And he said, "I know a bad situation when I see one."

An argument ensued, and I probably handled it badly, though I think the staff at the Escondido was equally to blame. As a result, my continued employment at the Academy is under discussion, and I have not seen or heard from Lee since then. While Pete Sampras is a well-known celebrity, I do not know if it is in your wishes for your son to be the hitting partner of a washed-up balding husband of a second-rate Hollywood starlet. I told him he would need your permission for us to let Lee go anywhere, and he said, "It's been handled," without explaining what that meant.

I believe great things are in the future for all of us provided we sort out these complications. Would you be able to come soon to Florida, or might you be able to meet with me where you are to discuss strategies? If you hear from Lee, can you tell him that we still have work to do?

I am waiting for your reply,

Maximilian Gross

Venerable Mr. Wilcox,

There is not much these days to say for loyalty, or for all the careers I've nurtured, or for the reputation I've developed over decades of playing and teaching and learning about the game. Around ten of the players stood up for me, as well as a few of the cafeteria staff, and Antonio from the pro shop. But then there were lies spoken by a few of the least reliable, those most likely to profit from my expulsion, those who would turn the Academy into nothing more than a way station to the pros. Gone would be any learning, or staring up at the sky, or listening to music such as your own. Gone would be the role of the imagination, so much larger in the life of a great athlete than most educators ever recognize. Go study the neurochemistry of Nastase and Panatta and Budge, and certainly Federer and the great McEnroe, and you will see so much of what you might see in the brains of Mozart or Degas or, from your world, Miles Davis. What if this side of those brains had never developed? It was my job, I always believed, to link the physical and the metaphysical. Now it will be repetitive drills and weight training.

I saw Lee after he'd cleared out of his dormitory suite. I had the sinking feeling one has when one has been lied about. At the same time he seemed as though he wanted something from me, something he couldn't articulate. Tropical storm clouds gathered above us.

Neither of us knew then about my impending dismissal, and I said nothing to him of my talk with the director. I gave him a signed copy of Brad Gilbert's book on match strategy, and enough string to last him through the summer.

"Did you steal this?" he asked me.

"Of course not. It's yours," I said.

"I'm all set on equipment," he said, the sky darkening. "But thanks for the book."

On the title page I'd written a warning about Sampras that I now wished I could erase: *Big serves are like big bustlines. Nice to look at, but no guarantee of a person's character.*

Nothing else was said, because it started to pour. I wondered what one does here—shake hands, embrace? In some measurable way my heart was breaking. We stood across from each other awkwardly and then he walked away.

The Danish girl has quit the Academy and has accompanied me on my trip north to see you. She is crazy about Lee, she says, and wants to meet you. I am devoting myself now to her training and believe she has it in her to make a splash at the Australian this year. I am not fond of the way people look at us while we're on the road, and so for now we are pretending to be father and daughter, like James Mason and Sue Lyon. There is nothing untoward about our interactions, though on one occasion Vivi, frustrated I believe by her inability to contact Lee, pressed her not unremarkably soft lips against mine, something that startled me and that I told her definitively could not happen again.

In the evenings, while she watches her TV shows, I've taken to long drives in no particular direction. I simply veer toward the empty road. Sometimes I play your music and listen to my own thoughts, and other times I break into tears for no reason other than that it makes me feel, oddly, loved. I try and remember the good things, matches I've won, people I've helped, a dog I once rescued from the pound. I think of walking the grounds at Wimbledon on opening day and praying it wouldn't rain.

Lee has been playing regional tournaments in California. I know this because I have a former player out there who has sent me emails about Lee's results. While he is winning matches here and there, I have no doubt that his progress has stalled outside the Academy, and I wonder whether Pete Sampras has the time to devote to him or whether he's simply found a third-rate coach out there to feed Lee balls. I wonder if there's a library out there, or anyone to go to the movies with. I wonder what happened to his friendship with the boy who smoked pipes, who I saw loitering around the Academy for a week or two after Lee left. I wonder about Lee's ability to so easily break his attachments, and whether that comes from the same place as your ability to end relationships

with the women you have been with over the years, though I know
I'm overstepping my ground here.

For the next week we will be staying at the Knights Inn in
Kalamazoo, Michigan. There are courts nearby at the high school,
and Vivi and I are out there training. Are you available early next
week? I would not mind at all making the trip to your house in
Grosse Point.

With hopes of seeing you soon,
Maximilian Gross

Mr. Wilcox,

I imagine you are surprised to see the postmark on the
outside envelope. But yes, in point of fact, I find myself living
productively and gainfully in Copenhagen, Denmark, thanks to
the efforts of Vivi and her parents, the Ingebritzens. They have put
me up in an apartment outside their indoor tennis club a mile or
so from the great Tivoli Amusement Park. I am now coaching five
young ladies and two young men, all of whom have some degree of
talent, the best being Vivi. I read somewhere that you lived in this
city for a year, and I wonder if there are any places you would have
me go in my first months here. I did make it to your house, you
know, though it must have been when you were in Los Angeles
visiting with Lee and the Samprases. Did they have you to their
ugly house? I find myself swinging these days from stretches of
loneliness and doubt to pockets of unrestricted happiness, and as
strange as it sounds I think I owe both of those moods to you. To
your music, your imagination, and your strange and gifted son. If
I never see him again, he will still live within me, as do you, Mr.
Wilcox. The Danish girl and I had a two-hundred-shot rally today,
and one nearly as long right after. I'm wondering how many times

early in your career you were in places like this, relying on your wits and your talent, and a woman who did not judge you, who trusted you when you'd forgotten how to trust yourself. I do not often think of Lee these days, but I hope he is in your life where he belongs. As you requested, I will not write again or try to get in touch with you or Lee, but know that you will always be part of my neurochemistry, the part of me that sings and mourns and deeply understands. This is what I've learned from your music, and from my coaching, and what I will continue to pass on to the Danish boys and girls, of whose talent I am sole guardian.

I am taking a Danish immersion class at night, and now when I dream I dream in Danish. When I wake up in my Copenhagen apartment, under my cold cotton sheets, I sometimes feel touched by magic, as though nothing in my life can ever go wrong. Do you know this feeling? Did you feel it when you saw your son hitting peerless ground strokes with the great Pete Sampras, and if you did, did you recognize the gift I'd given you?

Can we say that we are even?

Yours truly,

Maximilian Gross

JANUARY

My mother is dating a man named Russell who owns a boat with the words *Smooth Sailing* on the back. Russell has put *Smooth Sailing* away for the winter and he's trying to talk my mother into an all-day Nordic safari, maybe even a drive out onto frozen Lake Ontario, which on a day like today will feel like the Sahara itself, he says. He shows up at our house with his blue-tinted sunglasses and neon green ski jacket on, as though there's a ski lift in our house.

"If you're going to live in the cold, you may as well love it," he says, as if it's that easy to love something. Russell has a way of making you feel small because he does so many big things, like shooting the rapids and hang gliding off rocky gorges. He bounds through our house like a happy Lab waiting to go out and shit.

My mother is drying dishes in the kitchen, and though I can't see her, I imagine she is shyly smiling. Russell is what my mother wants, probably always wanted in some ways, like a trip to Europe or a house in the mountains.

"The Jeep's still running, babe," he says, and the word is a bug in my ear. Russell has snow in his hair and it's starting to melt, which makes it sparkle when the light hits it. He looks over at me. I am on the couch reading *Guitar Player* magazine.

"Come on and take a ride in the Jeep. The fresh air'll put some blood in your cheeks," he says, and I wonder if I look as sick as I feel. I would just as soon take a pass from December through March on all this outdoor crap. I haven't exercised much since I sprained my knee on Halloween and long walks tire me out.

My mother strolls out of the kitchen drying off her hands and pulling her long black hair out of the band she wears when it's just us in the house. She's wearing a burgundy fleece that Russell bought her and blue jeans. The two of them are dressed like the college kids I see at the coffee shop.

"The Jeep's still running. Let's go," he says to both of us, and I wonder if he thinks the thing will drive away if we don't leave in the next minute.

"Let's go, Dex," she says. "Have you ever been in a Jeep before?"

"Yes," I lie.

"Well, put something warm on and let's go."

I look at Russell but all I can see are those blue glasses and that square jaw and that smug toothy smile. I want him to jump in that Jeep and drive off to wherever he took *Smooth Sailing* and pick up people's mothers down there.

But I say, "Wait a minute. I'll be right out." And I grab my coat from my room.

It is January again. My father is watching television and dying. He's at Columbia-Presbyterian in New York City and he's watching television all day long from 6 A.M. until *Larry King*, which he'll fall asleep in front of. He used to watch TV with me when he lived up here in Oswego with us, but my mom got tired of all that nothing, she said, and kicked him out. He didn't threaten her, didn't swear, didn't even argue like he used to. When she asked him to leave, he said she was right to want that. He said it while *CSI: Miami* was on.

When he left, my mom gave all the TVs away so I've taken to reading magazines and playing games on my computer. There's not much else to do where we live, being that it's freezing cold half the year and I'm fifteen and too young to get into bars, which is what everyone else does. My mom says she'd rather I shoot drugs than watch TV, although that's not true.

My mom used to say it was the TV that made my father sick. But I said it was getting kicked out in the cold that did it. She asked him to leave in January and you do not want to know what January is like where I live.

It's close to zero every day and the ice mats in big chunks on the door so it's a hassle prying it open every morning, and the wind howls and whips through the piles of snow that cover our car and our mailbox and the red-and-white barbershop pole downstairs.

The day they fired my father we stayed in all afternoon watching soap operas and game shows. He ordered a pizza and said this was an opportunity, but it wouldn't last long and so we should enjoy this time together.

When my mom came home from work, he told her he'd been let go but it was all right, he loved us and that's what was important. She hugged him, but she looked desolately out the window, like an Iraqi war widow I saw on CNN whose husband came home with no legs. And I knew things were about to change. We watched movies that night until I got tired and went to sleep, but when I woke up at two to get a glass of juice from the fridge, he was in the family room, the couch surrounding his body like an old coat.

Something happened the day they fired him. He seemed content in the way calm people get when their bus is delayed and they figure complaining will do no good. He entered this funk in which he stopped washing or changing his clothes or eating at the table or bothering to sleep anywhere but the couch. And he watched TV. My mom says now she could see it coming on even before he got fired because no one gets fired for no reason, though it never seems justified when it happens to you.

He grew fat in front of the tube and he called about jobs a few times, but his heart wasn't in it. And when I tried to talk to him about it one night, he forgot my name for a full minute. He kept calling me Karl.

"I'm tired, Karl. Leave me alone for a bit," he said, each word slow and planned out.

"What's my name, Dad?" I asked.

He looked at me puzzled and then looked back at the TV.

"What's my name?" I said again.

"I know your name, now hush up," he said, calm, like we were in a library and he was reading a book.

"What is it then?" I asked. I wanted to hear him say it.

"It's Dexter, okay, it's Dexter," he said. But he forgot for a moment, and anyhow his brother Karl had been dead for twelve years.

He pointed his plate, smeared with dried salsa, at Hawkeye Pierce on the screen.

"You like this show, Dex?" he asked. And I said, "You know I do."

* * *

Russell's Jeep is humming now and the snow is melting off his defrosting windshield, just like it melted in his hair. Snow doesn't stick to Russell. He opens the passenger-side door and pulls the seat down so I can squeeze myself into the backseat. It's not really a space for a person, more for a toolbox or Russell's snowboard, but I sit lengthwise with my knees against my chest.

"You okay there, Dex?" he asks, but he doesn't wait for an answer and moves his head back out of the Jeep. The wind is so loud outside I can barely hear the music that's playing from Russell's stereo. The Jeep smells like cold clean air, the kind you earn by not leaving food or sweaty things around in it. Russell jumps in his side and he drops down the emergency brake. He runs his fingers up my mother's back and into her hair and gives her head a little scratch. Then he puts his hand on the gearshift and moves into drive.

The snow is falling and the road is sloshing around Russell's tires. There are only a few cars out and they are crawling, their drivers fearing they'd spin out if they went more than fifteen miles an hour. Russell's got a jazz CD in, the kind where everyone's trying to figure out what song they're playing, and he's acting like he knows it, wagging his index finger like a conductor's wand to the blasts from the sax.

Russell sells boats and rifles and fishing gear to sports stores so he's on the road a lot, all over the East Coast. It was Russell who told me my father was in the hospital. He knew because he was with us for Christmas and answered the phone when the doctor from New York City called.

The doctor said my father is chock-full of chemicals from the landfill where he worked, which led to his slowness and forgetting all the time. He also had pneumonia and some complications from that, but they aren't sure where the pneumonia came from. The doctor said my father is comfortable and is getting good treatment, which I know means he's dying.

When my mom found out, she cried a lot and she wanted to drive down to New York. But Russell said that would be "jumping the gun." I think the main reason I can't stand Russell is the way he acted the night of the call. He kept saying my father would get better and that we were lucky we had each other, as if he knew us.

"He wants us down there," I yelled at my mother. "You *owe* it to him. If he dies, it's on your head!"

At that my mother walked into her bedroom and slammed the door. I would have followed her. I would have apologized, maybe talked her into driving to New York, but Russell blocked my path.

"Dexter," he said. "Let's you and I go for a soda."

And so we did.

It was December 27 and all the lights were still up on First Street. The town was silent other than the hum of a thousand green and red bulbs laced over street signs and lanterns and dropped through the arms of short bare trees. Russell drove me in his Ford Taurus—his practical car—to the Ritz Diner, which stays open all night for the college kids and the all-night power plant workers and the winos who have no other place to go. It didn't seem like the kind of place Russell would frequent, but every other place was closed.

He had on a tight red racing sweater and did not remove his ski hat when we slid into a booth. We sat not talking for a while within the rustle of the diner: newspapers folding, a jukebox fluting, a waitress lazily clearing plates.

"You miss him a lot, don't you?" he said finally.

"Yes," I said.

"What kind of kid wouldn't want his pop around?"

He looked over my shoulder as he spoke. The owner of the Ritz, a red-faced man with a spruce white ring of hair around his otherwise bald head, approached carrying two menus.

"You fellows take your time," he said, opening them in front of us.

I sensed Russell was building up to something; he was going to lay his cards on the table. He rubbed his left eye, then flashed it four or five times as if finding the right focus.

"A boy needs someone around. He needs someone to look up to. I know that." He nodded his head. "But, mister, don't go riding your poor mother about that man in New York. He's put her through quite enough. She's getting her life on track again. Don't go throwing her off the rails."

He leaned toward me, over the table as though he might at any moment grab my collar.

"Listen, she can't remember a single happy memory about that man. All she remembers is him sitting around and driving her crazy. You want that again? Your father's been sick before. He'll be all right. It's part of his makeup."

He disappeared then behind his menu. All I could see was the top of his ski hat.

"What if he isn't all right?"

"Look, if it's serious, we'll get the news. We'll get you to New York. But it doesn't do any good to start imagining how the world's going to come apart."

Two women in the next booth were listening to our conversation. One of them, blond and with a pierced eyebrow and bright red lipstick, turned around quickly when I looked up.

The Ritz owner glanced over at us from the counter, where he was reading the paper, and Russell motioned him over.

I told Russell to order for me and I went to the men's room. I stayed there for fifteen minutes maybe, sitting on the pot, not doing anything but avoiding Russell. And when I walked out, he was eating a wet piece of apple pie and talking to the woman with the pierced eyebrow.

There was a half-melted ice-cream sundae at my place. I took a bite of it.

"Are you okay, Dex?" the woman asked, looking concerned.

It annoyed me that I'd been their topic of conversation.

"Yes, but I'm not as hungry as I thought."

"No one's forcing you, Dex," Russell said. "You can do whatever you damn please."

My mom is looking back at me as we push through town, by the stores on Bridge Street on our way to the lake drive. She wants us three to get along, to be a family. It's our chance to leave Oswego she says, maybe even upstate New York. Russell's company is headquartered in Florida, and he's due for a transfer.

There is a huge orange snowplow ahead of us spraying snow about. Russell flicks his wipers to full speed. He swerves side to side waiting for his chance to spring us out into the open road. Eventually the plow driver, a thick-bearded man in a blue woolen Giants hat, pulls to the side to let us by.

We're curving out on Route 104 along the lake, with the orange sun cutting down beneath the clouds, and I think about how long it's been since I've been outside, I mean really outside. I take in a couple lungfuls of air.

Russell steps hard on the gas pedal and the Jeep begins to bounce off the snow craters beneath us. "Yeeeeee haaaaaa!" he yells. He laughs and my mom does too, but she says, "You're going a little too fast."

"Anything you say, babe," he says, but he doesn't slow down. My knees keep knocking me on the chin, until I cover them with my hands and then *they* hit me—about once every twenty yards.

The lake flies by, endless and white. It looks less like the Sahara than the moon, pocked and jagged, and I wonder how long you could walk out on it and not fall in. Russell says he's driven twenty miles across, but I guess that figures.

The fish and hot dog stands are boarded up good, and the Rudy's sign is swinging hard on a rusted-out chain, slapping against the side of the building. The road narrows as we swing by the summer cabins that perch like gravestones on white lawns.

I'm thinking of my father driving Russell's Jeep. I'm thinking of him fidgeting with the gadgets, running this thing slow and deliberate as if it was made of glass. Russell isn't thinking of anything except how radical his Jeep is, though I might think that too if I had a Jeep.

With a burst of speed, we weave around a bend and my mom says, "Really, Russell. Slow down."

Russell says, "I am," and he whips his head back at me. "Am I going too fast for you, Dex?"

I say, "Yes," but he laughs like I'm joking, and he reaches over to his breast pocket. He somehow pulls out a cigarette with his right hand, sticks it in his mouth, lights it, and while he's looking down we hit a sinkhole and my head hits hard against the roll bar. There's a high drift in the road ahead and we swerve out of its way toward a utility pole. Russell slams on the brake, sending us past the pole into a spin, and I fall forward into the back of my mom's seat.

"Jeezus," Russell says. He has lost control. His mouth is open and empty.

"Jeeezus," he says again, and he's winging the wheel back and forth as though he's bringing a ship in during a storm. I've got my arms around the top of my mother's seat and she's holding her hands straight out into the dash. We are sliding fast toward a culvert. Russell is panicked. It's scary, but part of me is happy because Russell is fucking up.

We wash off the road, through mounds of snow pushed off by the blowers, and as we smack the bottom of the culvert, I bang my head in the same spot as last time. It's like a kick from a metal boot. I run my hand through my hair and I touch blood. The skin around the gash is puffed and sticky and my temples are throbbing.

Russell lets out a deep breath from his lower lip, which blows his hair up, and he takes his glasses off. His eyes are startling. They are gray and deep set, surrounded by white skin, where the sun's been blocked.

"Jeezus, you all right, babe?" he asks my mom.

She says nothing. Her face is ashen. She breathes hard and fast and the music is blaring now. I've still got my arms frozen around my mom's headrest.

"I'm sorry, Dex. You got the worst of that, didn't you?" Russell says. He breathes onto his blue glasses and wipes them clear with the bottom of his sweater. He turns the CD player off, then leans back to look at my head.

"It's okay, Russell," I say and pull away.

"You know we're really lucky," he says. "Really lucky."

And I guess he would think that, but I don't put much stock in that kind of luck. You could always say we could have died there and feel lucky until you die, but that's an idiotic way to go through life.

"Let's go home," my mom says, and there's an edge now to her voice. "Let's get this thing on the road and drive home." Russell reaches his hand around her shoulders and my mom tilts away, her eyes trained across the lake.

Russell's cigarette is burning on the carpet before him and he stomps it out, pounding his foot hard into the floor. My mom glares at him and then out the window again and Russell says, "Can you give me a break here?"

For a while my vision is blurred—glassy and dim, like film shot underwater. Then it is clear, but framed by moments of blackness like a slide show. I sit for a while in the snow, particles melting into my jeans, and I watch Russell and my mom moving around the Jeep, talking, plotting, their bodies appearing near me, then a few yards away.

The lake and the sky are the same white now and it is as if we are caught in a cloud. I look out over the ice and let the whiteness spread through my brain, the wind now a steady moan around my ears. I feel Russell's hand on my shoulder. "Come on, Dex. Get up and help us out," he says, and he reaches under my arms to lift me.

The motor is idling. My mom is in the driver's seat, and Russell and I stand behind to push. He has graded a wall of snow and dirt with his boots to keep us from sliding back.

"When I say 'Go,' move this thing into gear," he yells to my mom.

We count to three and then Russell yells, "Go! Go! Go!" and the wheels sound like buzz saws ripping through the ground. The Jeep climbs two feet and then falls, like a house, pushing us aside. The air around us is filled with fumes that seep inside my lungs and splotch the snow black.

"Let's try it again," he says. My head feels feathery and I am of no use here. I want to take a bath and go to sleep. The light is beginning to fade and the temperature has dropped a few degrees. The wind is snapping at our faces.

The two of us rock the Jeep up and back, up and back, and then, like we're charging a castle, we lower our heads and surge.

"Go! Go! Go! Go! Go!" And we get the front wheels on the road and almost the back wheels too, but it isn't enough. The Jeep pins us back into the snow and I am sweating now. Russell is exasperated. I know he's thinking it's my fault somehow; if it had just been him and my mom, this wouldn't have happened, which is bullshit. These things happen, even to people like Russell.

He digs in. "We got it this time, Dex," he says. "We got it licked." We lower our heads together, dig our shoulders and bent arms into the rear corners of the Jeep, and like two friends we push through the mounds of snow and earth. Everything is giving beneath us, the ground is moving backward, and Russell is yelling, "Go! Go! Go! Go! Go!" screaming now until the Jeep, wheels spinning wildly, mounts the culvert onto 104. My mom's momentum carries her a hundred yards down the road. She is whooping and so is Russell. He makes a snowball and hurls it at her.

I am covered in snow now, some of which has melted through

my coat to my chest, and my face stings from the cold of the spray and the wind.

"Hey, wait for us," Russell yells to my mom, and he starts running for the Jeep, his legs churning like the athlete at the end of the race, and I'm floating now on a wave of dizziness.

I am running light-headed, first slow, but then hard, and as fast as I can. It's the way I used to feel in gym after a long basketball game, strained, but alive, very alive. I can't hear the wind anymore and I can't see the cars or houses, just the white road in front of me, and I can feel the warm flow of blood on my forehead. I can faintly make out the Jeep's honk and my mom yelling behind me, but I'm running and I'm on my own and it's all I can do to keep from falling down.

STAY UP WITH ME

Henry is in the part of the dream where his father carries him piggyback through the shoulder-high waves. His father's T-shirt is soaked through, and the salt water is making the cut on Henry's elbow sting, when a woman's voice calls out, "Henry . . . *Henry*."

Before his eyes open he knows who it is. He can tell by the smell of her shampoo it's Alice. He'd been napping in the café around the corner from his apartment—the one open until midnight. "He just left," Alice says, sitting down at Henry's table, which is by the corner window.

She does this fairly frequently, finds Henry, now a boy-faced thirty-one, somewhere in the neighborhood when she wants his advice. Once—when she needed to choose between two job offers, she searched the grocery store, three coffee shops, and two bars before discovering him seated with his eyes closed on the couch at the Laundromat. Henry has been escaping into dreams a lot lately, in movie theaters or on buses or subways, but mainly in cafés or coffee shops where he spends the bulk of his afternoons and evenings reading or working on one of his scripts.

"He *thanked* me," she says with a pained smile. "Services rendered, I guess."

He stares at her blankly, then glances at his watch.

"I'm sorry to bug you. But I really *need* you, Henry."

She gives him the little-girl pout, the one that often convinces him to give her rides, or buy her dinner.

"All right, then. When did he come over?"

"Just after nine."

Henry does the math. It is eleven now. "Now *that's* 'efficiency.'"

"It's not like that. He works in the emergency room and he has this ridiculous schedule. Anyway, I think I was insensitive to him."

"How so?"

"His dog died this morning . . . I guess that's a pretty big deal."

"Yeah, I'd say so."

"I told him I was sorry, really sorry, *many* times over. I just . . . I don't know. I mean how many times can you say, 'My God, that's awful. That's so *sad*'? I had a pretty traumatic run-in at work and I just kept it to myself."

"Dogs are family members," Henry says. He gazes down at his screenplay, which is about a spy mission in Tunisia during World War II. He considers letting Alice read some of it, and then remembers how badly that went last time.

"He said it had a heart attack. Since when did dogs start having heart attacks? I thought of a dog dressed like one of those overworked executives—eating too many bacon cheeseburgers and keeling over."

Henry looks at the other tables to see if anyone else is hearing this.

"I'm going back to work here," he says.

"Not just yet, Henry."

"I've got a deadline."

"But you were sleeping."

"Napping."

She bites her lower lip and sighs.

"Do you want to maybe go grab a drink?" she says.

He considers the offer. Henry is in the parched badlands of a dry spell, and the thought of a couple of drinks with Alice followed by a trip to his apartment is like a sugar rush, apt to raise his spirits for an hour or so before dropping him into a prolonged crash.

"Maybe not."

"All right," she says. "Can I just sit here with you and read for a while. Remember when we used to do that?"

"Do you have something to read?"

"No."

Henry hands her a book from his bag, then goes back to working on his screenplay.

Alice begins reading the book and twirling a strand of her straight brown hair around a pencil. After a while she tilts her head thoughtfully and asks him, "How's your *dad*, Henry?"

"He's good."

"I think about him all the time."

Henry raises his eyebrows dubiously.

"Let's go visit him this weekend. Like we did that time. Remember? When we went to the movies afterward."

"Moulin Rouge."

They'd arrived ten minutes late and had to sit in the front row. With all the jump cuts and pulsating lights, Henry felt as if he might go blind.

"I thought it would cheer you up."

"You thought it would cheer *you* up."

"You were the one who was being strange."

"Water under the bridge," he says.

But Henry remembers it vividly. He was planning to ask Alice to move in with him that night after they made a lobby drop-off of some books at his father's. His father insisted they come up for a quick drink so he could finally meet Henry's *girl,* and his old-fashioned use of the word touched Henry enough to consent. He had assured Henry that his apartment was in "cocktail party shape," and possibly in his eyes it was. He'd set out a full bar—dusty bottles of Tanqueray, Stolichnaya, and Maker's Mark—a few wedges of odd-tasting cheese, some hard salami, and what might have been pâté, and he'd clearly vacuumed, and straightened the furniture. But along the most cursory of investigations, Henry saw trouble: moth-eaten alligator sweaters thrown over piles of paper in his office, mold growing on the refrigerator shelves and in the corners of the bathroom.

Until that night it was possible for Henry to live in a state of suspended judgment about his father's circumstances, but now through Alice's eyes he saw every coffee stain in the carpet or stray clump of rice on the kitchen stove as proof of his father's alarming decline. His father had downed a martini or two before they arrived, giving him the jittery, gin-emboldened air of a nightclub emcee trying to earn the love of an unresponsive audience. He told a few reliable old stories, told them flawlessly and then, like a man who takes the wrong road on the way home and finds himself on a street very much like his but which doesn't contain his house, lost his bearings. When he recovered, he warmed to Alice and acted around her like a teenager with a crush. She flirted back. It irritated Henry, though he knew it was simply her way of making herself comfortable in a strange situation. When Alice leaned down to retrieve a fallen ice cube, Henry caught his father admiring her ass.

When his father retreated to the kitchen for a forgotten hors d'oeuvre, Henry apologized for the mess in the apartment.

"It's fine. He's been the perfect host," Alice said, without knowing how true that had once been. In the old life, his parents' parties were legend: posh caterers, pianists and torch-song singers, and guests in black tie—all before the businesses tanked, and before his father fell asleep smoking a cigarette, burning two rooms of their brownstone—and before Henry's mother left, sending Henry plummeting into that blind alley of resentment where he both hated his father for making his mother leave and felt responsible for him in his fragile loneliness.

At the door, Henry's father pressed Alice's hand in his and told her, eyes moist, how much he loved his son and that Henry was all he had left in the world.

Then, perhaps losing his spot in time again, he apologized to them both about the fire and showed Alice the burn marks on his forearm and shin.

"How often do you see him?" Alice asked, when they were outside again on the street.

"Once a month maybe." The truth was closer to once a week.

"I really like him," she said, then added, "He's different from what I expected."

"How so?" Henry asked, but he knew. Henry had gone to blue-blazer private schools and his father lived on a nice Upper East Side block. She'd been imagining luxury, or at least a semblance of order.

"You look like him, you know."

Henry peered at his reflection in a shop window. He looked much more like his mother, he thought.

She said a few more nice things about his father, about his sense of humor and the first-edition books she'd found on his shelves, but Henry wasn't listening.

"I think we should move in together," he said.

She ran her finger down his sideburn as though he were an injured pet.

"There's an idea," she said.

Alice heads up to the counter now and orders a glass of wine and an espresso for Henry, so that he will stay awake with her. It is in this café that the two of them first met. It was after they'd both attended a screening at NYU, where Henry once taught a class for a former teacher of his who had pneumonia. Alice and a friend were talking about films in general and Henry offered them a few well-honed observations about Otto Preminger and John Cassavetes. Alice had long legs, ringlets of brown hair, and alabaster skin, with six small earrings circling one ear, and a little too much mascara around her large brown eyes. She seemed quite interested in Henry's opinions and countered with a few provoking ones of her own. She was slightly younger than him, twenty-five or so, and she had seen most of the movies Henry cherished and had read many of his favorite books.

Before long they were spending entire weekends at Alice's place, staying up until four watching underground films Henry brought home from his part-time job at the film archive, or just messing around, and waking at noon. Some nights they'd hit a party thrown by one of Alice's friends, but they rarely stayed long and sometimes, after a cocktail or two, they'd sneak off to a back bedroom, or a bathroom or a stairwell. They learned how to keep their voices down and their eyes open, and were caught only once, by someone who was too high to care.

One night, as they entered a restaurant for a late-night supper, Alice in a tight satin T-shirt and narrow black skirt, hair pulled back in a spiky bun, Henry lazily self-assured in the tan suede shirt Alice picked out for him, Alice's hand in his rear jeans pocket, he paused to imagine what they must look like in their just-fucked bliss: like the kind of people you'd die to be.

Henry's thoughts are floating in that time as he leaves the coffee shop with Alice and heads with her toward the blue-lit bar where they used to get tipsy together and make out. Henry hates the moment in which he wants her all over again, because it feels like regression, and so he treats her with a forged indifference, which he hopes will realign the balance of desire between them. They have far too much history to ever make this work, he thinks, but in certain moments, moments like this one, or on the occasional nights Alice decides to sleep over, he wonders. They are fluent in each other's faults and wounds and hypocrisies, and so sleeping together has the feel of sleeping with a failed part of themselves, like pornography with familiar dialogue.

He could teach a course on their maneuverings, he thinks, and yet he'd always get half of it wrong.

"There's no one I'm closer to in the whole world than you, Henry."

"I feel the same," he says breezily, before realizing it might be true.

He wants to tell her his theory—that the night at his father's had pushed them off course. Alice had witnessed Henry's future, or so he imagined, and so to alter that trajectory, she began needling him about finding a full-time job or selling one of the dozen screenplays he'd finished.

And she took heed of his subpar housekeeping, and his smoking, which Henry said he'd stop, but never did. He rebelled by smoking more, and allowing the plates to pile up. The question of their living together was never brought up again.

She asked him at a Burger King one night about his family when he was a kid, a softball tossed so he could give her something positive to hook into. He refused to describe aloud any of the happy scenes that he'd been playing over in his mind in order to get to sleep: the surf and turf barbecues, the Florida vacations, weekend parties on the Cape, rides in his father's white Mustang convertible, his mother reading him *Watership Down* when he was eight and to his thrill changing one of the rabbits' names to Henry. They felt too much like the right answers to an admissions interview.

"Like everyone else's," he said.

And then a more unsettling memory came to him, of when he'd actually last spoken to his mother. She'd called from Albuquerque, New Mexico, from the house where she was raising two other children with a different husband, to tell Henry she loved him, and always would. It was late Thanksgiving night. Her voice felt so close, he was certain she was just down the block. *"Henry,"* she said, as though it hadn't been five years, as though they'd just been speaking. *"Are you awake?"*

Alice waited for him to say something, anything, but he only glared at her and lit another cigarette, staring at the match like he wanted to set the place on fire.

They're drinking whiskeys now, seated across from each other in a booth. Alice smiles fondly. "It's so easy, isn't it?" she says.

"In some ways."

"Remember the things we did in that bathroom?"

"That wasn't me," Henry says.

"Funny. Well, he kind of looked like you. I was pretty hammered," she says.

To be truthful, Alice was never as drunk as she pretended to be, was always in control, and always looking, watching, grading Henry, or so he believed.

"Remember when we sat on opposite sides of the bar and pretended we didn't know each other?"

"That I remember."

"I kept sending you drinks."

"And then you made me pay you back."

"I guess I did."

Henry sifts his drink and watches how the ice cubes catch the light from the bar.

"I was such an asshole to you, Henry."

"Oh, I don't know. Who can tell about these things?"

"This was our place, and I shouldn't have come here with someone else."

It takes him a moment to realize what she's talking about.

He'd managed to put from his mind the afternoon she'd brought the ass-faced music executive here, and Henry had seen them through the side window.

"By then it didn't matter," Henry says, but it had made him crazy seeing them flirting (and ear nibbling) like a scene from early Alice and Henry. He got wasted at a dive down the block and then shattered the window of a black Saab 93, the model of car he'd seen the date and Alice riding in the weekend before. He used a rusted metal folding chair someone had left on the street. Utterly senseless, especially since the car Alice's guy owned was blue.

Alice leans toward Henry now and runs her hand from his temple across the back of his head. Her index finger brushes a lock of hair behind his ear. He feels very sleepy. She pulls his face to her and kisses his cheek.

"Let's go back to your place," she says.

On their walk to Henry's apartment, he thinks again of his father, and how rather than dismissing Alice's concern about his father, it might be better to tell her the chronology of events since that awkward visit, how Henry had put him in a managed-care facility, and how his father had become paranoid and frightened, but how for five full hours on his sixty-fifth birthday, his father had been himself at forty, and how he and Henry had laughed and reminisced together like lost best friends.

Alice and Henry hold hands up the stairs and as they enter Henry's clean apartment, it crosses his mind that maybe they could try things again, because it *was* easy in a way.

They sit on his bed and kiss, and then slip beneath the white down quilt. Alice asks him, "You don't think he's a lost cause, do you?"

"I haven't given up on him," he says.

From her confused silence, he realizes she isn't asking about his father. It stumps him for a moment, and then he remembers.

"Oh, right," Henry says. "He'll come back."

"Weird place to bring it up, I know. But I kind of like him. I didn't mean to be rude to him."

And then neither of them says anything for a while.

She places her arm across his chest. "You're so *good* for me, Henry," she says. "You really are."

He feels very tired, and then very cynical, like someone who buys a car and then learns the engine is dead. He turns into his pillow then and lets his eyes close.

After a while, he hears her softly whispering his name, "Henry . . . Henry?"

"What?"

She moves his hand between her legs.

"Do you want to?" she says.

"Let's go to sleep," he says, and turns away from her.

"I want to," she says, spooning him. "No one gets me like you do."

He thinks of booting her out, though he has neither the energy nor the inclination. The heat kicks on again with a clank and hiss.

He will move from New York, he thinks. There is nothing to keep him here other than his father, and he can come back to visit, and monitor his care by phone, from a distance—but he will not stagnate here another year. His father will be happy for him. He thinks of places he can go, Boston, or Los Angeles where he has contacts, and the sort of man he would like to be when he gets there.

"It's all for the best," he says to Alice, and tries to explain why, but in his sleepiness he loses the strand, nods off in mid-sentence, and drifts back to the dream: *A sand dune and the smell of seaweed. His tanned and healthy father carrying a bucket of mussels his mother would use for bouillabaisse. The cousins are over and in the back of the house Henry has built a fort out of milk crates.*

"Henry," the voice says again. "*Henry.*"

But he won't come back for her this time.

She keeps speaking, or maybe she's only speaking in his dream, but likes that he can leave her like this, that he can find a place away from her.

"I'm *sorry,*" the voice says now. It isn't Alice anymore.

"Say it again," he says.

"I'm so sorry, sweet Henry."

"Of course you are."

PARIS

Kistler's *second winter* in upstate New York was a season of fires, snowstorms, and deaths. There was a killing down in Granby where two boys, barely eighteen and flying on acid, shot an old man in the head. There were three stabbings—husbands and wives having problems—and a fire at Bodley High School that put seventeen children in the hospital. The gusts outside were so strong one of the firefighters was blown fifty yards through the air from a ladder. A priest in Albion was charged with molesting four altar boys, a seven-year-old was knocked flat between the frosted wheels of a '78 Cadillac, and an old woman threw herself off a bridge into Onondaga Creek.

Kistler covered the stories closely; he talked to the families and tried to stay clear when people asked him to, when they wanted to be left alone. But more times than not they told him what they were feeling and what they thought of a world that had come down so hard on them. They read his pieces at wakes, asked him to calling hours, seated him with grieving cousins and siblings. It was the poorest county in upstate New York, rural to the core, and still they made him feel like family. He was not a religious man, but there were times when his job felt like a calling.

In March, during a news lull on the cops beat, Kistler was moved to night meetings and features. They buried his work on the regional page and his mind started to drift. He'd begin an interview and then daydream. He'd be miles away and the person would be talking and then Kistler would see a hand waving in front of his face—"Hello," they'd say, "anybody home?" or "Have you heard enough?" He'd look at his pad and he wouldn't have a single quote. He might not have turned on his digital recorder. It was even worse at the meetings they asked him to cover. He knew what happened at these things was important, that a shift in zoning laws or problems at a sewage treatment plant were matters people cared about, but it felt too much like taking dictation.

In the office, when he was bored, he'd pore through a book that had been left by his predecessor in the bureau, a photo-diary by a Danish journalist with a long braided beard who spent five years in American slums with junkies, prostitutes, and transvestites. There were dark shadowy photos of couples shooting up in stairwells, two boys beating an old man in an alleyway, a sharecropping family with torn, soiled clothing squatting in the corner of a sloping shack. The book had a far-reaching arc to it, a design and scheme, and a beating heart, Kistler thought. It made his work seem trivial and pointless. This was the world the politicians had forgotten about. Kistler could not shake the feeling that he too was letting someone down.

* * *

The week after the county's budget talks—an edge-of-the-seat affair—Kistler got the idea to write town profiles, to roam the back roads of moribund hamlets no one ever bothered to explore. Most of the county was agricultural, but not everyone farmed. Migrants turned profits for a few wealthy landowners, but the smaller granges had foreclosed. The major industry had revolved around the rail lines, which died sixty years ago. In hamlets like Williamstown, Paris, and Albion, more than half the people were unemployed. Kistler wanted to shake things up, to depict a way of life few people ever saw. There was an important story in rural poverty, one the big media outlets never covered, one of neglect, isolation, and domestic violence.

He could see the harbingers when he pulled through town to the Paris diner: scarred paths overgrown with honeysuckle thickets, a rimless backboard in a weed-filled playground, two children hurling a ball where a hoop should be.

Inside the diner, four men in flannel shirts sat at a table in the corner, under a shelf of mildewed trophies. Northern European faces, Kistler guessed. High cheekbones, sturdy jaws. Kistler ordered a beer and walked with it over to their table.

One of the men smiled broadly, betraying his yellow teeth. Smoke rose from the table in curlicuing eddies that whirled toward a ceiling vent. The man cleared a space for Kistler.

"What can we do for you?" he asked.

"Oh, we're thinking of doing a story on the hamlet."

"Who is *we*?"

"The newspaper."

"What do you want to do a story on?"

"The town itself. Sort of a profile."

The men looked at one another and laughed.

A gaunt older man they called Joseph, around sixty, with

tiny blue eyes and two days of beard, took Kistler's arm. His fingers pinched like a clothespin below Kistler's shoulder.

"You're not going to dig up the fire stuff, are you?"

"What fire stuff?" Kistler asked.

"Never mind," he said. "Every five years or so someone comes out here and writes something about the fire."

It piqued Kistler, but he knew not to press just then. He took their names and he asked them about town lore, the early days, their grandfathers and town politics. They told him about the cheese mill, a shoe factory, two foundries, and an epic week-long blizzard ten years ago.

Kistler had the sensation of floating outside his body, watching himself with these men, shooting the breeze and sucking down a beer. What he should do to do this right is to live in the hamlet a while to get a feel for it. He pictured himself doing this, people gradually becoming more comfortable with him and taking him into their confidence. He wondered what their impressions were of him. He realized the man with the red face had finished making a point and he hadn't heard a word of it.

Kistler nodded. "I agree," he tried.

"You agree?" the man said. Kistler realized he'd answered wrong.

"You agree?" the man said again and snorted. "He agrees," he said.

Kistler rose from his seat. He pushed the smoke away. "Can I get anyone another beer?" he asked.

That evening Kistler e-mailed the photos of the hamlet to his editor with a note that read "Richest nation in the world."

It had been a month since Kistler's girlfriend broke things

off with him, and her absence had left him feeling disconnected and isolated. In the fall, when she was living in Boston and he'd gone to visit for the weekend, they'd agreed to make lists of the things they didn't like about each other—the issues they needed to work on. Kistler had been critical but honest, and he expected no less from her. They exchanged sheets and her page was blank with a heart on it. Kistler tried to grab his back but she kept it and read it all the way through. She said nothing afterward and even thanked him for his honesty, but it set them off balance.

Their habits diverged. She started talking about sea kayaking and cross-country skiing and bike trips she was taking with friends he didn't know. He was pale and tired, and exercise was something he could barely recollect.

Valentine's Day she called Kistler at the office and told him there was no point in dragging this out. She was spending the night with someone else. She then sent him back his sheet of paper.

Kistler lived in the downtrodden section of town in a one-bedroom apartment above a barbershop. He showed his parents the place when they visited and the look on his father's face seemed reason enough to stay awhile. "This is the way people live," he told his father. "The way you live is a completely foreign concept to people around here."

He heated the leftover lasagna he'd made over the weekend and turned the TV on to CNN. A reporter was speaking through the brattle of gunfire somewhere in Iraq. Kistler found his mind drifting to the men in the diner. He wondered if he'd made an ass of himself somehow.

* * *

In the morning Kistler interviewed Helen, a short, plump
woman with a thick swirl of blond hair, on the front steps of her
trailer. Under her coat her T-shirt hugged her stomach. The snow
whipped across her lawn like litter, spraying the windows, piling
at the plastic that gathered like a sheath around her antennae.

"I'm trying to talk to everyone, see where they work, how
long they've lived here," Kistler said.

"I don't work. I take care of them," she said, pointing to
the gang of children screaming and leaping in the snow. Kistler
guessed there were seven.

"How long have you lived here?"

"I don't know, maybe two years? Can we wait on this until
my husband gets back from the store? He wants to be in on this,
he said."

"I just need a minute. Can I come inside for a minute?"

She paused, looking Kistler over, and he saw his chance.

"Two minutes. It's no big deal," he said. She opened the door.

Once inside he scanned the living room: the red plastic
couch, the stuffed animals, and old dolls and board games strewn
about.

Helen poured Kistler a glass of coffee, and on the brown
couch in her living room he asked about the fire.

"They burned it down. They set their own fire department
on fire to collect the insurance—three of them from the department. Your newspapers went wild. A fireman committing arson
is big news. It got to be sort of a joke. I was in high school then
and they rode us about it pretty hard. And then there was the lice
business."

"What was that?"

"Oh, the kids had lice a few years back and they had to run tests on them. There are a lot of mean things people say about the place. You know, that we're arsonists, that our kids are having incest. When you grow up here you get used to thinking of yourself a certain way," she said. "Now I read a good deal, and I've got family in Rochester and Albany so I know different."

"Have you thought about moving somewhere else?"

"I really haven't."

"Why not?"

"Oh, you know. This is my home. I live here," she said.

"Of course," Kistler said.

Saturday, Kistler called the schools department to talk about Paris. The superintendent told him the lice story was true. He asked the county social services department about the unemployment rate and outbreaks of birth defects and incest. He asked a farm psychologist about sexuality in isolated areas. He called a teen pregnancy center to find out how many of their clients came from Paris. They gave him the number of a fifteen-year-old client, who he interviewed on the promise he wouldn't use her real name. He pulled old clips on the firehouse fire, gathered stats from Pulaski, another town near there, for comparison. The Paris General Store manager gave him the liquor and cigarette sales figures and told him about four men he knew who spent most of their welfare checks on lottery tickets.

He took quotes from an apple farmer who told him he couldn't get people in town to pick.

"I've got migrants that come in from Florida and Texas that

are making ten, fourteen dollars an hour sometimes. But almost no one around here will do it. They'll pack the boxes and I pay less for that," the man said.

The man told Kistler social services had become a trap for the people in Paris.

"If they work, they got to give the sitter eight bucks an hour, right? So in the long run they figure it doesn't pay," he said. Kistler wrote the quote down and put a star next to it.

The piece, when it was finished, was strong, Kistler knew. There were no quotes that weren't corroborated, no facts stated without statistics. He had not editorialized. And beyond all, the pictures were vivid. There was a shot of the diner, the regulars playing cards or laughing behind beers and plates of food. Another shot of the vacant factories and two of the trailer park. It was as compelling a portrait of rural poverty as he had seen.

When he sent the story in, his editor called him.

"This is staggering stuff," he said.

The story ran the next morning with pictures of the trailer park and the diner. Kistler's prose ran two full pages.

He would not have chosen the headline: "The Town Time Left Behind," with the subhead "No Springtime in Paris." A bit too flippant, Kistler thought, but the article was left mostly untouched.

At ten, the county social services director called to say his whole family had read it. "It carries an important message," he said.

Another reader from Syracuse called a half hour later. "Imagine living like that," she said. "And all those children. It made me feel a little more fortunate, I'll tell you that much."

Then a man from Paris whom he hadn't met called to say the paper had sold out in Paris, in Albion, in Pulaski, in Williamstown.

He didn't speak to Kistler. Instead he called the editor. He said the article pointed to a lot of matters that needed discussing and he invited "the reporter" out to an impromptu meeting.

The word spread around the newsroom that Kistler's story had caused a stir. The managing editor read it. The publisher looked it over. Every ten minutes or so Kistler's phone rang.

"I think a story about that meeting could go front page," his editor told him. "Especially if you've got some people hollering, demanding things from the town board."

His bureaumate, Marsden, pored through it, his feet on his desk.

"What do you think?" Kistler asked.

"I don't know, Kistler," he said. "You've got people talking about incest and arson here. They all sound like drunks."

"That's a fairly narrow read of it."

"I guess I'm narrow then."

On the day of the meeting, Kistler didn't shave. He put on a creased shirt with thin ridges of dirt on the collar and cuffs and old blue jeans. He took his own camera. It was an afternoon for pinks and blues in the sky and as he drove through the dead tan benchland, disked with corn skeletons and bare thin trees, he realized how focused he'd been the last week or so. It made him feel good.

The day had warmed and the cleared wet road caught the sun. If the meeting went more than three hours, Kistler would have to file by phone, which he didn't like to do. He'd done it at a drowning and people had eavesdropped on his description of the body he'd seen pulled from the water. It made him feel self-conscious and he edited himself more than he should have. The piece when it ran was flat and had none of the color of the moment.

The meeting was in the town's fire hall, a florid metal and wood structure that might once have been an airplane hangar. Next to a flagpole on the front lawn, a wide yellow sign listed Bingo nights. Kistler veered around the lot, which was clogged with pickups and cars, a dozen or so children's bikes with banana seats and thick-ridged tires. It was the biggest meeting Kistler had ever covered.

The air inside was stale, with thick curls of smoke passing through the beams of light, which emerged from two old-style spotlights in the back corners of the room. A podium stood at the center on what looked to be a theatrical stage. A man whom Kistler hadn't met in his previous visits walked over to greet him. He had a red-and-white-checkered shirt and new blue jeans, eyebrows that came together in a V, and tall black hair that gleamed with comb marks. His name was Mr. Thomas, he said, and he would introduce Kistler.

"People are kind of upset," he said. "But you can understand that."

Kistler nodded, though he did not know what he meant.

"I think people will appreciate the guts it took to come out here like this. By yourself, too." Mr. Thomas had a copy of the story in his hand and Kistler wanted to grab it from him. It felt like he'd stepped onto the wrong train and was heading far from his desired destination. When he looked out at the audience, he saw that nearly every one of them had a copy of the newspaper in their hands.

Mr. Thomas moved to the podium and motioned Kistler to wait to the side, near the American flag.

He poked the microphone until it sang like tires burning. Kistler saw the men from the diner in the front seats. They stared straight at him as if they could make him disappear with a good glare. In fact, it was all men in the first two rows, large and, from the looks of it, angry men in flannel shirts and baseball caps, and behind them were some couples and whole six-member families, children in bright sweatshirts fidgeting. He heard a baby cry and then somebody cough. And then it seemed as if everyone was coughing. He saw other people he'd interviewed.

These people hate me, Kistler thought. *Everyone in this room hates my guts.*

Mr. Thomas tested the microphone and then smiled unpleasantly.

"We've got the reporter here and he's going to answer our questions," he said. "I think we're quite fortunate he made the trip. It's not everyone who'd do it under the circumstances."

Mr. Thomas motioned with his hands and then stepped to the opposite side, near an exit. As Kistler walked up, the crowd talked among itself—a sort of angry buzz. The spotlights shone in his face and Kistler felt his flesh leap. His left eye twitched slightly and he took his glasses off to rub his lids.

He pitched forward, feeling almost dizzy, and before he could speak a woman toward the back stood waving the article.

"My children were teased so hard in school they called me up crying," she said. "We are not a town of lowlifes and building burners."

The crowd whooped and hollered. Someone called Kistler a son of a bitch. A young voice demanded that he recant. Kistler started to reply and the man yelled, "Just do it, you little prick!" and rushed from his seat. Someone pulled the man down and held him.

Kistler let his pulse settle and composed himself, breathing deeply, and the crowd quieted. He spoke in a calm, flowing voice that felt apart from him. He talked about purpose, about why he went into journalism, his sense of the world's inequities, his role in their ultimate reversal. He told them how little he was paid, how a lot of jobs would have put him in cushier circumstances. He talked of roaches and mice in his apartment, and the long hours he had to put in. He said he apologized if he upset anyone but his job was to get to the truth.

The old man from the diner stood in the front row, clearly drunk. He staggered and then his voice came out slurred and high pitched. He steadied himself and then began again.

"'No Springtime in Paris'? Do you think we're *funny*?"

Kistler said he hadn't written the headline. He said parts of the article had been changed. As he spoke, the man with the red face stood, then two others. He saw Helen and a huge man, who must have been her husband, standing near the door.

Mr. Thomas walked over to the microphone. "All right," he called out. "You've made your point. We're trying to say something about the community here and you all are acting just like it says in his article."

Kistler wanted none of Mr. Thomas's defense, which he thought was an unfair read of his work. As Mr. Thomas stepped aside, Kistler whispered to him that he'd come expecting a board meeting.

He spoke into the microphone again. "I wrote what I wrote because it's what I saw," he said. The lights felt stronger now and Kistler had trouble focusing. A photographer was taking his picture. From where? he wondered. Who knew about this?

"I've always written what I saw," he said. "I know no other way. I am your voice, don't you see that? I-am-your-voice. If you're angry at me, you're angry at yourself. Your own life." The crowd was silent now, and Kistler felt empowered, like an evangelist. "You can wallow in this. Attack me like you're doing or you can strike out and make good lives for yourselves. Strong, caring, important lives of purpose. No one is given anything in this life. Life doesn't just come to you whether you're rich or poor, black, white, whatever. You find it. You grasp it. You make something of it."

About ten people clapped. The rest remained silent.

"That's all I have to say," Kistler said.

He walked out the side door. Mr. Thomas stopped and thanked him under the pale blue light of the parking lot. Kistler felt he'd dodged something huge and uncontrollable. Sweat ran cold on his face, and he felt flushed.

He sloshed through the mud and snow of the lot toward his car, which was beyond the glow of the lights, passing two teenagers and a woman in a long coat who wanted to ask him something. He pretended not to notice them. As he walked behind the firehouse, he realized he'd left his jacket and car keys behind at the podium. He saw Mr. Thomas pull away in his blue Mustang and others follow and he felt a deep sickness like nausea hang in his stomach.

He thought of abandoning his car for an hour or two and trying to find a place to hide out in. Every place was closed and he was very cold. He had the feeling he had lost something that he could not yet identify, but that he would know later, the way people do when it's too late and their decisions have led them where they would never have wanted to be.

He stepped through the soft ground around the building to the side window and peeked through. He saw only a small group twenty feet from the podium talking about matters that had nothing to do with him. He moved stealthily for his jacket, then walked quickly out the door again.

When he made his way through the lot again under the full yellow moon, he felt a hand on his back, fingers curling at his collar. Two cars had boxed him in. His heart raced, and his hands balled into fists. He turned and the woman in the long coat stood with her arm around a teenaged girl. The girl looked frightened, an infant animal on a highway.

"I just wanted you to meet my daughter," the woman said, and she stood back, away from the light. A man in an army jacket stood watching alongside a lanky boy resting against a car.

"She's a National Merit Scholar. She's got herself a full scholarship to Notre Dame University," the woman said. "She speaks French and Latin and she grew up in this town."

For a moment Kistler couldn't place himself. He did not know what he was doing out in the mud with these people. He glanced back at the firehouse and remembered. And then the girl began to speak in a foreign voice, in what Kistler guessed was Latin. It was like nothing he had ever heard. It sounded to him like a benediction. He began to shiver. As the girl spoke, Kistler's hand reached up and gently touched her cheek. It was as warm and smooth as sunlight.

SPECTATOR

When *I was twenty-five,* Abby was seven. When I was thirty-two, she was fourteen. This is something I dwell on, though I know it isn't constructive.

She is more worldly than a lot of thirty-year-olds I know, more so than my ex-wife for instance. Abby is comfortable with herself, comfortable with me, and still I see myself meeting her at a playground when I'd just married Lynn and started my life. Abby's in overalls standing near a swing set and I'm in a rented tuxedo, watching her.

For nearly two months Abby's been living with me and we almost never step out unless we have to. I teach painting at the college on Wednesdays and build furniture in my house, and Abby's looking into grad school. Anthropology or psychology. She wants to see the world, which I'd like to do with her if I can save up the cash to make it happen.

* * *

It is inhumanly cold here in Ithaca, and the streets are sheets of ice. We haven't seen the sun for seventeen days, which means we have to find ways to keep indoors interesting. Like playing strip backgammon or downloading music from places like Iceland or Tunisia or making five-course dinners. Or inventing games. We tell the life stories of bit characters in the movies we see, then compose new story lines for them in which they get rich, or end up in prison.

She is only nineteen, but I'd swear she's lived longer than me, or just learned more from staying up reading every night, or writing letters to her future self. ("It isn't a diary, I *hate* diaries.") She is nocturnal; daylight unnerves her. If she goes out in the morning to get us coffee, she wears my Blue Jays hat, tipped over her forehead, and a pair of sunglasses.

Abby says I'm the first one to get her talking about her messed-up past. I open her up, she says. We start our talks when it's been dark a few hours and we've eaten dinner, drunk some wine, maybe smoked a little weed. Then she says something that sends me spinning; never fails.

One night last week, Abby made some tea and put a Sigur Rós CD on and told me a story about a crazy aunt who lived in Montana, painted landscapes, and eventually hung herself, and she caught the woman's voice and gestures disturbingly well, shaking like an old lady and then easing into a calm, low-voiced drawl.

Her body is so damned perfect, even, or especially, with the ten extra pounds she's put on living here, which have softened her edges. Her skin is pale and freckled on her shoulders, and under her light green eyes. I watched her speak as she moved her arm in drunken brushstrokes, and when she looked at me, she fell silent, as though sorry she'd told me anything. Again, I felt like a voyeur.

"Go on," I said. "Keep going."

She said, "I don't want to. Let's go to bed."

Another night she told me how she spent a summer living on a beach. Not in a house near the beach, but in a sleeping bag with her sister and her mother on the beach in Isla Vista, California. And they begged food.

Picture this. We're eating a huge meal of eggplant lasagna and sharing a ten-dollar bottle of wine and she's telling me about begging for food because her mother figured she could store up the welfare checks and take a trip.

"We got taken in a few times, and we snuck into a house for two weeks," Abby says. "It was furnished and everything, with a big-screen TV, and art on the walls, but we didn't turn anything on unless we had to. We snuck out the back door when we heard a car pulling in and that was that."

She showed me a Polaroid of her and her sister, about seven and eight, waking up in a big blue sleeping bag, with their hair matted against their faces and their mother sitting next to them, wearing sunglasses and smoking a cigarette.

I started thinking about where I was that summer: twenty-five and dropped out of college. I worked that summer painting and rehabbing houses with my father. But what if I'd decided to drive out west like a lot of people did and I'd seen those three sleeping on the beach? What would I have thought?

That was the summer I fell in love with Lynn and locked myself in Ithaca for another ten years.

"Where would you go now if you could go anywhere?"

"Somewhere warm and cheap," she said. "Somewhere like Mexico."

Like someone's grandfather I wake at six, and I start in cutting and shaping wood. I'm building a rocker this week; I'm smoothing the spindles with a sander and I'm setting the headboard on the stiles, which are perfect this time, not too thin or too blocky. This was supposed to be for the owner of my favorite bar but I'm thinking of giving him a different one I made over the summer. This one is Abby's.

My workroom is spacious and drafty, with hardwood floors covered in wood chips, paint, and dust, which holds the room's light, like gauze. My father built this house, along with five or six similar ones in this town, big rambling things with front porches, fireplaces, and shingled garrets on top and high ceilings and mullioned bay windows, the kind of places that look instantly old and cost half your paycheck to heat. While I work, Abby sleeps, eight feet up, twenty feet away in my loft. She snores. She's the only woman I've known who does. I can hear her sometimes in the kitchen, but I never tease her about it because I know why she snores. Her mother broke her nose five years ago in a fight, a few months before she died. I'm the only one who knows that.

Abby says we fucked each other to death in a previous life, that it was written on our tombstones. She's joking, but it would explain a lot. I have never before been so lost in something like this, where it can happen at any instant in any room without notice. But Friday night, after we've been kissing and working things up to a high boil, Abby switches the rules on me. She pulls at the end of my belt and then as if remembering something, she lets it drop. We're on the couch in my living room.

"You think we could go a night without doing this?" she asks me.

"A whole entire night?" I ask, smiling, and I reach back to touch her thigh.

"I'm serious," she says. "Let's see if we can. Let's see if we can sleep in separate beds. Cold turkey. Twenty-four hours."

"What would that prove?"

"That we don't need it," she says. "I want to prove to myself I don't need this."

"I need this," I say.

As I said those words I wished I had them back.

Abby sinks under her hair. She stares down. She's wearing a plain white T-shirt and cutoff army pants, and she is painfully beautiful.

"Maybe that's not so good," she says. "Maybe it's not good that we're putting everything on this right now. Maybe I should stop missing classes."

"Let's not play this," I say. "I mean, I want to be with you and there's no reason we need to take a test to find that out."

"Let's just go one night, one lousy night without sleeping together and then we can go on every other night doing whatever we want."

For an instant I'm angry. I'm asking myself why I'm with a teenager; why I'm playing high school games instead of living with an adult.

Something shifts between us, or did a while back. I tell her she can have the bed; I'll sleep right here.

"It's just one night, okay?" she says, and she kisses me on

the nose like I'm a child. "We're not going to die or anything. You'll see."

From two until dawn, I pace by the loft watching Abby sleep. It is exactly like being dead, being unable to touch her. I watch her knees bend to her chest and her face brush the pillow. Her nose, curved and long, is dormant above her mouth, which is open to let her breathe. Her lips are chapped, and her hair is wild across the top of the bed. She's wearing the same T-shirt she wore the last three nights, a long College Town Bagel shirt with a picture of a bagel.

I'm thinking of all the places she's slept in, growing up around California and Boston and upstate New York. Her father died when she was two, and her mother was a little crazy. No one lives on a beach with her kids or moves ten times in four years unless she's crazy. The time Abby's mother broke her nose was when Abby moved her stuff to her friend Vicky's house. Abby said she'd forgotten most of what the fight was about, but it had something to do with her mother's boyfriend.

When her mother found her, it was ten days later, and her mother was so drunk she embarrassed Abby in front of Vicky's parents, slurring her words and cursing and then breaking down in tears. She lost all control is what she did, and she knocked Abby straight on with the base of her palm. Abby said it felt like her nose had been pushed back through her head. Blood poured over her T-shirt and her jeans and her bare feet, she said, more blood than she'd ever seen, and she couldn't breathe.

"Other people's mothers don't act like this," Abby said. "Other people don't have mothers who break their noses." She was fourteen when it happened.

* * *

I felt so sad and empty when she told me that, though I know if she'd grown up happy, she'd likely be sleeping in a dorm room right now. I wonder what her mother would make of me, closer to her age than Abby's. She probably wouldn't care.

I want so badly to climb into the loft with her. But she's taken control. It's my house and she's directing the show. I can't sleep. I'm watching Abby, and the sky outside is pale with new light.

Saturday, I take her out to see Liz Phair perform at Cornell. We drink a pitcher of margaritas and smoke a joint before leaving and Abby is real physical, running her hand over my leg while I drive. Last night is forgotten. The sidewalks are saffron from the streetlamps and Friday's snow. Not a star to see, the sky is gray and fierce.

She smiles at me like a little girl, like the girl in the sleeping bag. I can hear her wheezing hard through that broken nose, and I try to get my breath to match hers. For a minute or so it is just the human noise of one imperfect breath, two broken bodies working together. I feel a warmth rush over my head.

"What are you thinking about?" she asks. I stop at a light behind a van filled with kids staring out the window. One presses his nose into the glass and turns his head sideways, which Abby doesn't see. She is looking at me.

"How good life is," I say.

At the theater we play the overview game. Abby and I eavesdrop or spy on people and try to size up their lives from their faces, their arguments, their clothes. We sit at diners and watch old couples arguing, or new couples awkwardly ordering breakfast after they wound up somehow in bed together. We lay bets on whether they'd make it to a third date, or a fifth. "I'm betting he blows her off on the fourth date, comes up with a phantom stomach flu," Abby would say.

We walk along the second-floor railing, looking down on people buying drinks, posturing, talking. People are young here, high school and college, woolen caps and piercings. There are a few older earth types and the teaching crowd but I don't see anyone I recognize.

"He's driving her crazy," Abby says.

"Who?"

"That guy in the gray T-shirt. He's driving that woman crazy."

The two are talking to another couple.

"Look where she's standing. Look at her hands," she says.

They're clenched in balls, okay. And the man in the gray T-shirt has his shoulder just past her so he can't really see her while he speaks. Yes, I can see that. We stand watching. The woman from the other couple touches the man's shoulder while she speaks to him. He laughs.

"What do you think she's telling him?"

"She's complimenting him on something, it looks like," I say.

The woman, the gray T-shirt's date, pulls up closer to the other woman, leaning forward like a runner pushing for an inside lane. Then the two guys start talking, as though there's no one else there.

Abby's look says *Can you believe this?* And then I realize I know these people. I don't say anything. The guy in the brown suede blazer—I think his name is Daniel—says something to the group and then walks over to the line by the bar. Abby takes my hand and squeezes it. And then, this is what amazes me. From the bar, Daniel looks straight up at Abby and grins.

She smiles back and then turns away.

"That was strange," I say. "You know that guy?"

"I don't think so," she says, but a chill runs through my chest. What does that mean: *I don't think so?* Daniel's look is the kind a guy gives someone he knows, maybe slept with. I glare down and watch him order his drink and rest his elbows on the bar, and when I turn toward Abby, she is walking slowly away.

When Liz Phair, pale and wispy, takes the stage, I drift into a funk—torturing myself about Daniel. I don't hear the music; I just see him. I remember where I know him from, high school. He was a year behind me, bright, loud, and into politics. He played in a band, I think, and his father taught at one of the universities, which is what I think Daniel is doing now. That and getting a Ph.D. in something. It's amazing what you can remember when it comes down to it. I don't know if Abby knows him, but his grinning at her silences me.

I imagine him meeting her at a Cornell party, Abby in ripped jeans and a thin white T-shirt, and this pretentious fuck rattling on about art and music, while people around them hold wineglasses and tilt their heads thoughtfully. Then he takes her to his apartment where as a prelude to hooking up they listen to our music and tell each other our stories. That's what kills me— they talk in our voices.

Later that night I dream I'm with Abby, and we run into Lynn. Her hair is streaked with blond highlights now, and she's clearly done time at the gym. She has a child in tow—things have panned out for her—and she looks at Abby and says, "My God, Willie, she's beautiful. She's young but she's absolutely beautiful."

I say, "I know. We're living together now," and Abby turns her head away, declining her role in this. I say "This is what I wanted" or something like that, and Lynn's kid starts untying my shoe. I'm telling him to stop and Abby starts walking away. I run after her, diving on her eventually, and when I wake up I'm kissing Abby and holding her tight, though she's still snoring and smelling like sleep.

When I shift on top of her, legs around her stomach, she whispers, "*Easy, cowboy.* I'm not going anywhere."

I'm thinking of Daniel when Abby tells me her friend Carl is having a breakdown, and she's thinking of spending the weekend at his house, do I mind?

"What's the problem?" I ask, trying to sound trusting. I can't imagine that analyzing Carl is what she's longing to do.

"He's just got a lot of pressures. Too much to live up to. He's got no one else to talk to."

I know Carl. Carl was in the painting class I taught last fall at the college, the one where I met Abby. He is stick thin and pockmarked, and he drew ghetto scenes of New York, where he grew up, long-bodied men and women with exaggerated features. He is someone who I imagine has crises all the time.

"Well, why don't you ask him to come here," I say.

"Sure, if that's okay with you," she says.

"Let me think about it," I say, but there's no way I'd let that fuckup in my house.

"I'm losing my friends," she says. "I'm losing them because

I'm not ever seeing them. It's starting to get to me—being *here* all the time."

"Let me think," I say. "Sure. Do what you want." I'm pouting. I'll be thirty-seven in less than a month.

I go back to work on the rocker, and I listen as Abby talks on her cell phone.

"Hi, Carl," she says, and she tells him she doesn't know about the weekend. She laughs a lot and tells him to eat well and take care of his body and she gives him a list of breathing and relaxation methods to work on, rib cage out, shoulders back, and some yoga chants that she'd taught me. "Rama, Rama, Rama," and then, I couldn't believe this, she starts singing to him on the phone. The voice is like a ten-year-old's, singing high-pitched, third-grade songs: "The Muffin Man," "Frère Jacques," the *Brady Bunch* theme, and I feel like I've caught her in bed with someone.

Last summer I saw Lynn's wedding announcement in the Sunday *Ithaca Journal.* There was a photograph of my ex in a white gown, looking very pretty, like it was her first wedding, and next to her was a stout, long-haired man in a morning coat, a real estate broker from Syracuse named Evan. I was amazed at how little I felt. It was as if I'd barely known her, as though she were some girl I'd hung out with a half-dozen times.

If pushed, I can remember her being high-strung, doting, and as determined to talk through our issues as I was committed to avoiding them. We stayed together four years, two of which I stayed true and never went out much and the others where I rarely came home before 2 A.M., and I'd sleep on the living room sofa. It was the period after we lost our baby and everything shut in on us. She got pregnant in our second year, and for a while it brought us close; it really did. I built a crib and a high chair in my workroom, and I thought about ways in which we could make more money as she got bigger and went to sleep earlier than me every night. Things weren't perfect between us, but I thought being parents would ground us in a good way—rid us of the threat of possibility; I am not good when I have too many options.

I read in a book that only 2 percent of pregnancies that make it past the sixteenth week end in miscarriages. Lynn's happened in the twenty-third. The doctor at University Hospital said our baby just died, "aborted" was his word. He spoke like a man who has had children, and he said there would be nothing to keep us from having one "down the road."

Then he put his arm around me and told me Lynn would be fine, we would have each other and that's what was important, which is what people always feel the need to say.

It was the start of a period in my life in which I stopped paying attention and walked around dreamy and not in myself. I thought about trying again, about talking about things other than our pregnancy, which had so dominated our life. I grew quiet and I found ways to get out of the house. I did this, although I never blamed Lynn for anything.

When I stopped sleeping with her, she left me notes and a DVD, which I was supposed to watch, and she asked me to go with her to see a counselor she'd been seeing at the college.

I went once. He said it seemed like Lynn and I wanted different things out of life, and I agreed. He scheduled us for a Flexibility Workshop he was holding that weekend, and I drove instead to Albany, where I stayed with my friend Neil for a week. Neil has never married.

When I came home again, Lynn had moved out. It took

about two months to set up our wedding and four years to work out a divorce. We argued a lot but I think we ended well, no hate or anything—just piles of paper to sort through.

I thought of calling to surprise her and congratulate her, and I thought, *No, that's going backward, move ahead; concentrate on what you have.*

I tell part of that story to Abby—the part about not moving backward—by saying I want her to spend the weekend with me and not Carl. We'll book a cheap flight and head off to the Yucatán. It isn't her fault, I tell her, but Carl should know not to call her like that.

She says he's my friend that's all, he needs me like you need me. I say I'm sorry but that's how I feel. She says she can't go to Mexico, she's failing school. She says she's spent so much time at my house she's failing three out of four classes, do I care?

"More than you could ever imagine," I say.

"No, really. I'm *losing* myself with you. I'm giving so *much* and I'm not getting anything back. I look at someone or I talk to someone on the phone and you freak. You change, just like that, and you don't talk about it. We talk about *me* and all *my* problems but I feel like I don't know you."

And while she speaks I watch her hands move and her eyes flare and her chest push forward in breath. I can see her knees and part of her thigh beneath her ripped jeans. I imagine us in fifteen years. I'll be fifty-two and she'll be my age now, teaching at a junior college or a high school, somewhere like California. I'll have gray hair and an old-man paunch, and Abby will look like an adolescent boy's fantasy of a hot professor, a copy of Proust or Emily Dickinson tucked under her arm.

"Really," she says, and steps back from me. "Tell me something. Tell me something you never told anyone."

So I tell her a story about stealing money from my dad because I wanted to go to New York and how he found out and decided to take me down there himself on a Greyhound bus, which makes her happy and soft again, though it isn't true; I never stole a thing.

Before I take Abby to Carl's house, I take her to a thrift store on Buffalo Street to buy a pendulum rod and bob I saw there. If she's going away for a couple of days, I tell her, I am going to finish a grandfather clock, something I want to do before I'm forty.

"I'm not going for a month or anything," she says. "I'll probably be back Sunday night."

She has my motorcycle jacket on, my sunglasses, and a pair of my sweatpants, and I'm thinking of what my house has become. We haven't done a dish in two weeks and the sheets are thick with dust and sex, and it occurs to me I could whip the whole house into shape over the next few days. It might improve my state of mind.

The sky is gray and low as I crest the knoll by two small farms down from Buffalo Street; silos decaying, empty of corn, two bales of hay sitting there like junked cars. It is gray for so long where we live, you forget what spring is like, that it will even come at all.

When we turn onto College Avenue where Carl lives, Abby rests her head on my shoulder.

"Thank you," she says.

She has a pair of ice skates tied together at her feet and when I look ahead at Carl's house, a jaundiced two-story student building, I see him in front with his own pair.

I pull the car into his driveway and Carl walks over to Abby's side.

"What's up, Willie?" he says.

"Nothing, Carl. Nothing but clocks and snow."

He looks at me puzzled, and then hugs Abby hello.

As Abby walks into Carl's house, I'm thinking about sticking around, about hanging out with Carl and his roommates around a bong and some music. We'd order out a pizza, maybe watch a basketball game, which I like to do sometimes. But my sense is that Abby doesn't want me there.

I'm starting the car and driving toward Homer through the thick gray air, which has frosted with light snow. The farther I drive, the clearer it gets.

I picture them bounding down the hardened playing fields to the hockey ice, which is empty now because the team is away. They'll be swirling around, holding hands maybe, and making circles in the dim light of the rink. She'll be singing those songs again, grade-school songs, like a music box that you wind and wind, and then let loose.

I open the windows now and let the cold air in. I drive north for a long while until it's dark out and I can't recognize any of the town names. I turn off my headlights then and gun the engine and I think, *This is what it feels like to be lost.*

BIRTHDAY GIRL

A young girl lies on a snowy country road. Her head has fallen to the side as though she's sleeping, and her hair fans out across the snow. She is clothed in a blue parka with a white fringed hood, a red knit scarf, frayed jeans, and dark blue snow boots. She's alive, thank God (her breath warm enough to melt snow), though unmoving.

I never saw her, you tell yourself. She'd been running in the cold night with her dog, who sprints up and down the road, barking. You were rushing a little, to score some Advil before the market at the gas station closed, but really, the girl came from nowhere. You are banged up yourself, a cut on the inside of your lip, and shaking, and the scene emerges before you in pieces: dog/girl/car/snow/scarf. You can't wait for it to settle, for now there is getting the girl to a hospital. You don't own a cell phone to call for an ambulance. You will take the girl yourself.

But loading the girl into a compact car isn't easy, as you are five foot three, and in your doctor's words, *small boned.* Straining, and chanting profanities under your breath, you manage to drag and then slide the girl—who looks to be around fourteen, but weighs as much as you—positioning her with legs bent and head ducked down, so that the door can close without hurting anything. You recall too late the rule about not moving someone when they're injured.

The dog, you think then, because you can't just leave him out on the road like this. You yell, *Here, boy. Come here, boy*, to no effect. You grab a slice of chicken from the plastic container of your dinner leftovers and hold it out in your palm. He walks over, dragging his leash, and eats from your hand. *Thatta boy*, you say, and then wrestle him into the passenger seat of your car. He has a blue bandanna around his neck, same shade as the girl's jacket, and tan-colored fur. You try to calm yourself down.

In ten minutes or so you reach the emergency room entrance of the hospital, which lies at the eastern border of what they poignantly call downtown. You run inside and shout, "Can someone please help me? There's a girl in very bad shape. She's been hit." An attendant with greasy blond hair tied back in a rubber band rushes out with a metal gurney. He braces the girl's neck, places her carefully on the gurney, and rushes her inside.

You follow with the dog. There is dried blood on your hand, which you rinse clean at a water fountain. A few people smile over at you when you sit down in the waiting room. They think it's *your* dog.

Eventually a young man in faded green scrubs with a chart in his hand emerges. His sentences come forth in disconnected sounds: The police dropping by . . . a report.

You give him the sequence of events. A flash of something in your headlights. Brakes. A skid. A crashing sound. It doesn't feel like you're slurring your words.

"So the dog was running ahead of the girl," he says.

"I guess. I didn't see either of them." If only you'd hit the dog, you think. But it's good you didn't hit the dog.

"Where were you coming from?" he asks.

You consider telling him the truth, that you were in a bar, but because you ate at a restaurant called Howell's on Montgomery Street earlier, you decide to simply say "Howell's." You were with two friends, talking about your week of housesitting for your boss, who was on vacation in the Florida Keys. You liked staying in a place with leather couches, a nice sound system, and shelves of clever movies. Even now you're wearing her stylish red wool coat.

"Did you have anything to drink?" he asks.

"A glass of wine," you say, and surprisingly enough that seems to satisfy him.

"One," he says, writing this down, and you say, "Yes."

People are rushed in, one woman crying in pain and others with small or invisible bruises and limps. A TV plays Fox News, a story about a man donating his kidney to his brother. Beneath the television, a waist-high plastic Santa stands behind a pack of small plastic reindeers. There are other Christmas decorations still up, and a small fake tree adorned with little red ribbons. A young boy asks if he can pet your dog, and you say yes.

"What's his name?" the boy asks.

"Max," you say, the name of a hamster your father gave you when you were six.

* * *

You consider calling one of the friends you'd been to dinner with, but it's late now, and they are likely both asleep. There was a lawyer you dated a few times last year, but you'd lost his number, and that had ended awkwardly.

As you wait for the doctors to evaluate the girl, you are waiting too for the blood levels in your brain to shift, though you can't tell if it's alcohol that's causing the dull ache in the front of your head, or if it's an aftereffect of the collision. There is a formula that has to do with your weight, what you've eaten, and how many hours have passed. You recall seeing a chart about this a few years ago on a bulletin board at college, with the message A GOOD TIME TO MISPLACE YOUR KEYS. Your mouth feels dry. It's hard to swallow. You drink a cup of weak coffee from the dispenser in the waiting room and take several long sips of cold water from the hallway water fountain.

It's no big deal to drive with a few drinks in you, not in a town without traffic, where you can down a few shots of Patrón at a place like Finnegan's or The Orchard and still make it home— people do. You've had far wilder nights and been fine, although once after a party you did scrape a curb, and after another you pulled into the wrong driveway.

On a dare when you were thirteen, you once told four separate store managers it was your birthday—though it was still months away—and that no one in your family had remembered. You were so convincing in your disappointment (your eyes were disturbingly red) that you walked home that night with a compact disc, two T-shirts, a poster, and a beautiful silver necklace with a locket, which you are wearing now. It was alarmingly easy to do. The key was tricking yourself into believing it. You think of this as you think of what you'll say to the police.

At the sink in the women's room you splash cold water on your cheeks, then pat dry your face with a paper towel. You look like you always look. You have no record of unsafe driving, not even a speeding ticket.

An image through the windshield flashes in your mind. The girl's eyes are less scared than bewildered, as though she'd seen not a car coming at her but a UFO.

"You all right?" There's a woman at the next sink; you don't remember her walking in.

"Fine," you say. "I thought I lost a contact."

After a second coffee you feel more jittery than sleepy, and nervous, though this doesn't distinguish you from anyone else in the waiting room.

You can be whatever you need to be here, which is something you've always been good at. It was your inborn empathy, your drama teacher said. You'd starred in three plays in high school and another in college for which you'd earned a fawning write-up in a regional newspaper.

For now you focus on your role here. You locate a plastic soup bowl and fill it with water for the dog. It isn't much, but it feels good to watch him drink.

A couple in their midforties wearing heavy coats and scarves arrive and run to the desk. They have kind faces, you think, and are tightly gripping each other's hands. You recognize them from when you worked as a cashier at the Price Chopper. You realize you've seen their brown-haired daughter before, and vaguely remember slipping her a packet of gum her mother had denied her. The girl was eight or nine. Her mother had been fumbling through her purse and didn't see the exchange, but the girl's face had opened into a smile. At that thought a chill crosses your skin. You consider slipping away now, but then the nurse is pointing the parents over to you, and you rise from your chair.

"Thank you so very much for driving Eden here," the mother says, and then glances at the dog, "and look, you brought Lemon here too."

The parents thank you for driving their daughter to the hospital and for taking care of Lemon. They are so appreciative you realize they don't know anything more than that you might have saved their daughter's life.

You tell them how you worked at the hospital as a candy striper in high school, mostly in the pediatric ward. And then you report what little you've heard about the condition of the girl.

At some point in the conversation you tell them—because you *have* to, and because you figure you are as sober sounding as you are likely to be—"I'm the one who hit your daughter."

Your declaration confuses them.

"I'm so sorry. She came out of nowhere. I never saw her."

"It was *you*?" the father says.

"I'm so sorry."

"Dear God," the mother says, and she sits down.

"It was all ice out there. I wasn't going very fast."

"You were going fast enough," the mother says. "How long have you had your license?"

"I'm twenty-three," you say.

"Then there's no excuse."

"No, you're right. There isn't," you say. "I wish more than

anything in the world that I could do something. I wish I could go back wherever she is and do something." You feel yourself growing upset. "I really don't want to bother you. But I'd like to stay here until Eden wakes up."

The father studies your face, then looks over at his wife. They are registering the fact that you look quite a bit like their daughter.

"I want to make sure she's all right," you say.

He purses his lips and nods.

"I'm just so *very, very, very, very* sorry this happened," you say, close to tears.

His expression softens. "I believe you," he says.

A doctor emerges with an update for the parents. The good news, he tells them, is that the CAT scan showed no skull fracture and no evidence of internal bleeding.

"She isn't awake yet," he says, "but her pupils are reactive, which suggests she might simply have a concussion."

"So she's going to be all right," the father says. He's trying to read the doctor's face, which reveals only an affable competence.

"We'll have to wait and see. There could be some things the CAT scan didn't catch," he says, and adds that they may need to take her to another hospital for an MRI. They'll have to keep watching her closely.

Eden's left kneecap is shattered, he adds, probably from the impact of the car, and her left shoulder *was* dislocated, "but we did a pretty good job of putting it back in place."

The father nods. "We appreciate all you're doing for us," he says, and from your seat you nod too in thanks.

* * *

It is a record night for accidents, someone at the nurses' station says. Already there have been three other serious ones in and around town, including a fatal, which is why the police are so slow in getting here. If enough terrible things happen out on the roads, they may forget about you, though you know it's wrong to hope for this, and really, all you want is for everyone to be fine and healthy and sleeping in a bed, which is where you should be right now. Your headache has eased and your buzz feels weaker now, almost not even there.

Over the next hour and a half there is a heart attack and a bar fight, more people being wheeled in, and more waiting. You talk with the girl's parents about Eden, who they tell you is an accomplished gymnast, swimmer, and amateur comedienne. She performed stand-up at a school talent competition. "She'll have some good material about this," her father says.

He is a short sandy-haired man with the build of a wrestling coach. His eyes pucker at the corners with appealing little wrinkles. You think of your unnervingly handsome father who left when you were eight, and who'd stop in on the odd year to take you out to dinner, then ask you to pay half, or for all of it, explaining in a fatherly voice that he would pay you back next time.

"She goes out every night with that dog, for an hour or so," Eden's father says. "She likes to get on the back roads past the edge of town and let Lemon find their way back. One time they were away until midnight. A force of nature, that one. She's going to need some rehab, I guess. Maybe a lot, but she'll be better than ever after that. One of our others I'd worry about, but not her."

It would be nice to have someone worry about you, you think.

"I'll bet you're a great father," you say. It feels as though you're auditioning.

"Not always," he says. "But it's kind of you to say that."

By two thirty they still haven't heard anything, which the father says is a good sign. If it was bad news, they would have already heard by now.

"Do you think that's true?" the mother asks you, as though you know about these things.

"I think so, yes," you say, because there's no reason not to believe it. You kneel down and rub Lemon's belly, and he makes high-pitched happy sounds in response.

It is the sweetest family moment you've had in a long while.

At around three A.M. the mother tells you you should go home and get some sleep, and come back later in the day when Eden is awake if you would like. The mood is hopeful, though no one has come out to give you an update. The police arrive, finally, and ask you questions about the accident. Their faces show the strain of a difficult night. Perhaps it is because you were talking warmly with the girl's parents when they walked in, or because the dog is resting his head on your lap. Or maybe they're bad at their jobs, but it's all quite casual. They take down your phone number and address, and they leave. Nine out of ten times they would have administered a Breathalyzer. This is the tenth time. When they're gone, you almost feel disappointed.

You ask the father where Eden wants to go to college.

"She's only a sophomore," he says, "but she has her sights on Tufts. She's got the marks to get in—or maybe she'll go to Holy Cross like her big brother."

The fact that she has a big brother seems like a good sign. You picture him talking to her on the phone the morning after a miserable date, the way your brother used to do for you. And now he'll hear all about the girl in town who ran into his sister.

"But she drove me to the hospital," Eden might tell him.

If he's at all like your brother he'd answer, "I still don't like her."

There is a room somewhere where the girl is lying with IVs connected to her, and her body is fighting heroically, or struggling, and this is your doing. You want to find her now and tell her that you're sorry. You imagine the scene like one in a TV drama, with you as a flawed but sympathetic character, pretty in an unmemorable way.

You go to the lunchroom and buy a packet of Lorna Doones from a vending machine. You eat one under the droning of the fluorescent lights and throw the rest away.

At close to four you volunteer to take Lemon for a walk outside. The streets are silent until a snowplow makes a wake of slush on its path across town. Has it gotten warmer? You think of heading home. But what would you do? It's too early to call anyone, and there'd be too many questions. As the dog bounds ahead, you imagine the heady privacy of these walks with Lemon and what the girl thought about in the hours she was out of her parents' house. You did this in high school studying for parts, lost yourself in a stranger's life and not only in rehearsals, for whole weekends. There was a magic to it. Method acting, your teacher called it, but it wasn't acting. It was another way of being, a better path. You can guess where the girl would go, to the park behind the middle school, or the yards near the abandoned glove factory, or to the cemetery, where you would go with your friends to get high. You used to believe this place would kill you if you never left. Then you fled for college in Boston. You came back to take care of your mother when she was sick, and with her dead now you will leave again soon. If people ask about your father, you say he's dead too, because you don't know where he is.

You walk a mile or so in the white with the dog bounding ahead and the moonlight glinting off the snow, then halt abruptly when a car heads at you from the opposite direction. A block away the car turns, and when it's gone from sight you think: *I need to get back there*. The wind loosens a clump of ice from a nearby tree branch and it hits the ground like a box of dropped dishes.

You jog and then run the mile back, into the hospital and over to the nurses' station. Lemon tugs at his leash.

You ask, "Is there any news . . . about Eden?"

You hear the pleasing sound of a child laughing, and then realize it's the television.

"Oh dear," says the nurse, who began her shift when you left on your walk. Her accent is from the islands, someplace like Barbados. She says compassionately, "Nobody went to *find* you?" because she believes you are the older sister.

"Beautiful *girl*," the nurse says, and clucks her tongue. "Was it a hit-and-run?"

"Yes," you say.

"Well, I pray to God they get him."

In the waiting room Eden's parents are conferring with one of the doctors. Your brain shuts off, and there's a tingling in your arms and hands.

Years from now, on vacation with your husband and six-year-old son in Hawaii, you will make friends with a psychologist and find yourself more comfortable with her than you are with anyone in your everyday life. The psychologist will be traveling from Canada with her own family and staying in a bungalow a few hundred yards down the beach. Things will have turned out well for you on many fronts. You will be having drinks with her at dinner one sultry night and you'll slip and say that there are things no one will ever know about you. The psychologist, on her third mai tai, will joke and say, "You mean the sweet little child you killed once." It will be a terrible coincidence—a macabre line put out for no reason other than that she hadn't felt like doing her job on vacation. She will read your face and then switch the subject. She will slip you her card the next day and say she works by phone if need be. You will want to tell your husband that night, but then you'll wonder how he would feel about the fact that you kept it from him this long. You will ask him to drive for the rest of the vacation. You will fall asleep in your son's bed twice that week, with the boy in your arms. You will try to forgive yourself. Home from Hawaii you will pull an old man back from the curb, though in truth no car was speeding toward him, only a slow-moving cab a few hundred yards away.

Bless your soul, he will say.

* * *

The doctor in the emergency room catches your eye now, and purses his lips, the way you've seen in hospital shows, and once in a dream about your mother.

"Go and be with your parents," the nurse says.

It's as though she's asked you to leap from a plane in flight.

"Go on in there, dear," the nurse says.

They gaze up at you with unreasonable kindness. You plummet toward them, into the purity of their grief.

THE WOMEN

A *week after my mother died,* my father and I went to a series of holiday parties. We lived in a sixteenth-floor apartment just off Central Park West, and in our building alone there were four different gatherings at which you could see my father surrounded by an infield of swooning women. He had become, in the wake of my mother's death, desirable real estate, a handsome fifty-eight-year-old with money. He was testing the waters, and you could see it bringing him back to life.

One of the women he met took him to her personal trainer; another took him clothes shopping to stores like Kenneth Cole and Hugo Boss "to raise his spirits." He returned home weirdly pleased with himself, as though he'd regained fluency in a language he hadn't studied since high school. I'd borrow a new leather jacket of my father's when I went out for the night and I'd find business cards in the pockets, or a napkin with a phone number. Before long the women were dropping by our house, and I'd see them late at night drinking coffee in my mother's kitchen, moving in or out of the bathroom or my parents' bedroom, where they'd often stay over.

There'd be a scarf or a purse left out on a chair. I'd hear a woman whispering as she snuck out, for my sake, early, before seven. My room was next to the front entryway, and I was having trouble sleeping in those days.

For the first few weeks of February, my father dated a chatty frizzy-haired woman named Leanne who worked at the mayor's office scheduling press conferences and talking to reporters. They ordered in Chinese food, and they'd leave the half-empty containers lying out on the counter. They watched movies in his room, and then at some point his door would close. I pretended a few times that it was my mother in there, that she'd slipped in without my knowing, but usually I put my earbuds in to keep from hearing anything.

One night toward the end of that month, he brought home a woman from Los Angeles named Chloe who owned a string of boutiques and wore sparkly eyeliner, low-waisted jeans, and a belly button ring, in winter. She flirted with me when he left the room, quizzing me about my personal life and once touching my knee. She gave me her business card, which listed the address of her New York store. "Come by sometime," she said, with a predatory softness in her eyes. When my father walked back in, there was music I knew he hated booming from the study.

"This okay?" he asked.

"Oh, Steve," Chloe said, "we can do better than that." She went and turned the tuner to some kind of lame diva dance music. She started grooving on her way back.

She was about forty, I'd say, but she tossed her hair and gyrated like an extra on a music video.

My father glanced at me and raised his eyebrows. I wrote

ABSURD on a piece of notepaper and flashed it quickly so she wouldn't see.

"Both of you come here and *dance*," she said from the dining room.

She looked misplaced vamping next to the long oak dining table and under my grandmother's crystal chandelier. My father moved his shoulders tentatively to the beat. Chloe yelled, "Show your father how to dance, Andy."

"He does just fine for himself," I told her.

I went and hid in my room. When I ventured out an hour later, his door was closed, and I saw her satin jacket and a shiny red purse draped over the reading chair in the living room.

Later that same week, I watched my father pick up the widow of one of his business partners during the intermission of *Into the Woods*. They were sharing notes about the New York City Ballet, and she said she had no one to go with, did he know anyone with extra tickets? She came back with us for drinks after the show, and my father put on an old Billie Holiday record my mother had loved.

The widow's name was Patricia Hobson. She was an interior decorator and good-looking in a preppy, older-woman way, with attentive eyes, a long thin nose, and a long wiry neck. I kept staring at the cords on her neck as she spoke.

"New York is a fabulous place to be a boy just out of college," she said.

"How so?"

"Well, the ratio is entirely in your favor. There are so many gorgeous, stylish women in the city. I see them absolutely everywhere, and they're all single. My lord, Andrew, they'll eat you up. What's your type?"

I shrugged.

"He likes tall ones," my father said, because my last girl-friend had been my height.

"Well, my daughter is five five, but she can wear heels."

"I'm pretty sure I'd be a disappointment," I told her, and she glanced over at my dad and smiled kindly. "I doubt that very much," she said.

She started to size up our apartment then, commenting on the arrangement of the chairs and sofas and the artwork on our walls. "This apartment has so much potential," she said. "Give me a few hours some Saturday afternoon, and I'll show you what we can do."

"Let me show you something," my father said. He poured her a scotch, and they stepped out on the terrace to look out at the lights across Central Park.

"Oh, boy," she said, which is what everyone said when they saw our view.

"This is my favorite spot in the world. If you look through the binoculars, you can see people jogging around the reservoir."

"I run around that reservoir four days a week," Mrs. Hobson said.

"Let us know next time so we can watch for you," my father said. I thought he was joking until I saw his face.

"I will," she said. "We can wave to each other."

I slipped out later to get drunk with my high school friend Jonas, but the whole time I was picturing my father and Mrs. Hobson ransacking our underachieving apartment, taking our keepsakes down to the storage lockers in the basement of our building. There were legitimate grounds for my fear: in the last week two framed photographs and four drawers of clothes had vanished. I think my father wanted to disperse my mother's ghost discreetly and respectfully. But every couple of days something else was missing, most recently a picture of my mother and godmother as teenagers, resting on a hammock like lazy goddesses. In its place now was a blank spot on the wall.

It's got to stop, I thought.

Jonas tilted his head, puzzled. I guess I'd said it aloud.

"He's not cheating on her," he said.

"Because she's dead, you mean. I suppose that's technically right." We chugged our beers, then Jonas went to the bar to refill our empty pitcher.

"I have a friend who wants to meet you," he said when he returned. "Actually, she's a little obsessed about it."

"What did you tell her?"

"This and that. You just come up in conversation, and then it's all she wants to talk about."

"She must have an exciting life."

"She does, actually. She's really smart."

"Good-looking?"

Jonas paused, as though I'd asked a trick question.

"Sort of. She kind of hides it. She doesn't do much for me, but maybe she would if I didn't know her so well."

"You told her about my mother dying?"

He nodded. "When I told her, she cried."

"That's just too fucking weird," I said. I reached for my father's jacket, which was on the floor next to me, and rested it on my lap.

"It wasn't." He put his cigarette out and lit another. "Anyhow, get comfortable, brother. You're not getting anywhere near that apartment for another couple hours, you got me?"

When we finally made it back, we saw her coat on a hanger in the vestibule. Jonas ran his hand across Mrs. Hobson's scarf and then bent over to smell it.

"Your dad is outstanding," he said.

I took a tin of sour candies from her coat pocket, just to do it, really, not because I wanted anything of hers.

Both my father and I were in therapy then. He went two mornings a week to an animated man named Bergman who had a book-lined office on the Upper East Side, and on Wednesday nights I saw a woman named Dr. Helendoerf down in the Village. Bergman and my father started meeting shortly after my mother was diagnosed—at my mother's urging. When my father left therapy, he seemed uplifted, which was far from the case with me. He and his therapist talked about my mother, probably, but they also talked about art and politics, even sports. Bergman was constantly finding his way into our breakfast or dinnertime conversations. "Bergman thinks the Mets should trade Piazza," he'd say. Or "Bergman gave me a list of Polish films for us to rent." They were friends. I once saw them walking down our street together, which seemed like a violation of the patient-therapist relationship. I asked Dr. Helendoerf about it. I asked her if she would ever take a walk with a patient.

She tilted her head slightly to the right. She wore a neutral pashmina that resembled the ones my mother wore.

"Is that something you think you would like to do, take a walk with me?"

"No," I said, too emphatically. "I mean, not especially."

She allowed a long awkward silence.

"Why do you think you asked, then?"

I didn't have an answer. I began to hear a buzzing sound like a halogen light turned too high or low.

"Do you think perhaps you're disappointed sometimes

when the world doesn't respond to you the way it responds to your father?"

"That's probably true," I said.

I saw her write something down.

"But I don't want that kind of attention."

"Then why do you think it is that you're so angry?"

"I'm not angry," I said.

She didn't respond. She might have raised her eyebrows.

"I just don't get why he's so happy all the time."

She continued to study me. I was fairly used to these stand-offs. In the silence, the buzzing started up again.

"Do you hear that sound?" I asked.

She paused for a moment. "What sort of sound?"

It was faint now, and probably from somewhere on the street.

"I guess I don't either," I said.

When my mother was sick, I was out of the house a lot. I'd go out to work—an entry-level job I'd talked my way into at a public radio station—and then I'd stay out until everyone was asleep. Once I stayed away for nearly two weeks without telling anyone where I went. I missed her birthday party. When I reached my father on the phone, he was madder than he'd ever been. And then he forgave me, which was even worse. He said I was distraught, which was true, but for the longest time I just felt numb. He said people cope in different ways. He said he thought of leaving all the time, which I believed and didn't care to hear. I couldn't really say why I needed to be away, and really I was able to put my mother out of my mind most of the time.

Dr. Helendoerf said I was repressing my reactions to my mother's illness and "obfuscating" my emotional responses. And she said that was a big reason why I stayed in the house all the time now; I was trying to keep my family intact by staying at home. I told her that was bullshit, if not in those words.

I called my father to see if I should pick up dinner, and a woman answered the phone. "*Aw, fuck,*" I said, and hung up.

On my way into the building, I was spotted again by Mrs. Wiederman, a gaunt red-haired woman who, like four or five others whose names I forgot, invited me to dinner every time she saw me.

"I made a pot of stew you can keep in the freezer and heat up for your suppers," she said, whispering to protect my pride.

"We're eating out mostly," I said.

"Well, I'll just leave it outside your door, then," she said. Dishes in sealed Tupperware, aluminum pans, and plastic Baggies had been dropped off on our doorstep ever since my mother died.

"You know your mother would be so proud of you," she said as we rode the cramped and ancient elevator together.

I thought about the arguments my mother and I'd been having over my lack of direction.

"Why?" I asked.

She seemed confused by the question.

"Because you're a lovely young man," she said. She stepped toward me then, held my face in her cold damp hands. I smelled mouthwash and old-lady perfume. Then I felt the walls of the elevator shiver. She was actually going to kiss my face.

"Get away," I said, pulling back. "Did you even know my mother?"

She gasped, and then stared at me with her mouth open, as

if I was dissolving before her eyes. "Oh . . ." she said. "Oh, dear." When we got to her floor, she stumbled out of the elevator.

"And we don't need any more of your shitty dinners," I yelled.

I felt pretty bad about this later.

As we made our way across the park on a Saturday to the Metropolitan Museum of Art, my father told me I hadn't been myself lately. We were walking through the Seventy-Ninth Street fields, by Belvedere Castle, and in the cold our voices came out in vapor. "I'm fine," I said. "And you?"

"I know you're not sleeping," he said. A man in a gray Columbia sweatshirt jogged by, with a black Labrador keeping pace.

"It's getting better," I said, though it wasn't. Whenever I dropped off, I kept having a dream in which my mother was alive and the two of us had to go around convincing everyone we knew that she hadn't died. "Prove it's you," they'd say. She'd tell them their middle name or their birthday, and they'd tell her she had gotten them wrong.

"It's a strange time for everyone," my father said.

We stopped on the path, facing each other. I smoothed a patch of dirt and stones with my foot. The buzzing in my ears was constant now, like the static on a radio station that only partially comes in, or a wiring defect on a speaker you might eventually get used to.

"It isn't my business," I said, "but it might be easier if there weren't so many of them."

"You're right," he said, and sighed. "I need to slow down."

"What the hell, you're living," I said.

He considered this for a moment. Then he put his arm around me like I was twelve again.

In the track-lit lunchroom of the museum, my father was his old self again. He told me how he chased my mother to Europe. He talked while a waiter with a white shirt and black bow tie poured us Heinekens, tipping the glass to keep down the foam. He met her on a Memorial Day weekend when she was a waitress on Martha's Vineyard, then met her again when she was checking coats at a party in New York.

I'd heard this story so often I used to groan when he started, but not this time.

I wanted him to slow down and tell every detail.

"She'd rented a house with your godmother in Nice, a two-story cottage with a yard and a view of two churches and a bakery. I couldn't stand being apart from her," he said. "I took my three weeks of vacation and flew to France. She didn't know what to make of me. We barely knew each other, and there I was, on her doorstep in my shorts and T-shirt with the Michelin guide to Italy and Greece under my arm, like a college kid."

He took a sip of beer and cleared his throat.

"Two weeks later, in Venice, I proposed. She was probably the most beautiful woman I'd ever met," he said. "And far and away the most perceptive. It's like she'd lived a thousand lives because of all the books she read. It sometimes made me uneasy."

"How come?"

"Because I couldn't hide the way I could with other women." I could hear him breathing, heavy and slow.

He held my glance, then put on his glasses and studied the check.

"You remind me of her sometimes," he said without looking up.

That night, for a few hours, my father appeared genuinely haunted, and I was heartened. He sat in his study looking out the window for a while, and then he took out some files from the cabinets in there. He was flipping through my mother's notes and preliminary pages for her book on Paul and Jane Bowles.

For all my father's achievements, my mother was always a step or two ahead of him. She was the one who'd finish the Sunday crossword puzzle, who knew word derivations, who could speak three languages, who had more persuasive things to say about the films and plays we went to. She feared alternately that I would pursue success single-mindedly like my father or that I'd inherit her impractical intelligence, the kind that ensured the vibrancy of their social life but that only recently had earned her—in the form of the Bowles advance—even a modest income. When she was on her deathbed, I was still deciding who to be like, and who to rebel against, though I still had time to fail them both.

I watched him from the doorway. I felt a bit guilty for forcing him into my mood, but it was a mission I'd undertaken.

"Someone should follow up on this," he said. "All this good work shouldn't just go to waste."

"Maybe I will," I said.

His eyes lit up. "Oh, I'd love that. I really would."

Then he gathered up the pages, put them away, and got dressed to go out.

* * *

The radio station was on the fifth floor of an old warehouse building on the Lower West Side. I had to call from a pay phone to get someone to open the padlocks on the back door and bring me up in a rusted elevator. I assistant-produced for a phone-in issues show (the insurgency in Iraq, corruption in the Justice Department), screening callers and gauging people's on-air skills. Their politics didn't matter to me, so long as they had something to say. The most intense conversation I had was with a man whose wife had Alzheimer's who'd called to talk about stem cell research. After forty-five years of marriage, his wife barely recognized him, and once, after a meal, she tried to tip him.

I listened to his stories, and then I told him about my mother. Nothing planned. He spoke and then I did, back and forth, a game of catch. I told him about lying to everyone, making excuses for her thinness. That was her rule. She thought her publisher would cancel her contract if it got out that she was sick. I told him about Thanksgiving, how I kept pushing her to eat. She said politely she didn't want any more, but I insisted. She couldn't hold it down.

She covered her face and ran to the kitchen, my father and me hovering as she leaned over the sink. *My God, I can't do this. I just can't do anything.* She was so terribly sorry, she said, that she'd ruined our Thanksgiving. "It was the last time we ate a meal together, and I screwed it up," I said.

"You're lucky." The caller had an even baritone and a slight Brooklyn accent. "You're more than lucky she's dead and buried. Dead and alive is what's killing me. It's breaking my heart."

* * *

Jonas met me at the Dublin House on Seventy-Ninth and Broadway later that night. It was packed, and everyone was drinking as if the end of the world were coming; at least it felt that way to me. We settled down at a dark wood table in the back and made our way through two sizable pitchers. I described how my father appeared to have a steady girlfriend now, a school administrator named Linda.

"Women do great on their own," he said. "But the men from our fathers' generation are kind of clueless. For all their yelling at each other, my dad couldn't go three days without my mother. Remember when my aunt Beth died? My uncle Ned remarried within five months. . . ."

The buzzing in my head started in again, and then the music got incredibly loud. Jonas was saying something about the way we're wired, which I couldn't really hear. Then it felt like someone had shoved cotton in my ears.

"I've gone deaf," I said.

He helped me to my feet and pushed me through a maze of beery faces out the door. In the freezing air, my hearing returned.

"Is it possible you're working backward through the healing process?" he said.

"Fuck off."

"I'm not knocking it. I think it's admirable."

I threw up on his shoes and felt somewhat better.

Over that weekend Jonas took me to a Rites of Spring party on Spring Street, endearingly enough. We rode the subway down, then walked there through a late-March blizzard. The cars moved soundlessly down the street. From somewhere in the heavens a snowball scraped the top of Jonas's head.

"Took you fucking long enough," a woman's voice yelled. She was leaning out the window of a fourth-floor apartment.

"Took us forever to shovel out the driveway," Jonas yelled back.

The party was packed with downtown hipsters, most about five years older than us, with something already to show for their lives. In what passed as a dining room, the snowball hurler, Sylvie, was arranging the hors d'oeuvre platters and mixing margaritas.

"You're Andrew," she said, when I walked by the food table.

The crier, I thought.

She handed me a margarita, then tucked a strand of hair behind her ear. She was nearly my height, pale and possibly sleep deprived, with an oval face, soft features, and dark brown librarian glasses. When we shook hands, hers was damp from the snow, or from squeezing limes.

After a minute or two of introductory conversation, she said, "I'm really sorry about your mother."

"Thanks," I said.

Someone called her name, and she excused herself and went to hug a woman in a short skirt and knee-high boots, who introduced her to a white guy with thick dreadlocks.

When she returned, she said, "I don't know if Jonas told you, but I went through something similar when I was in high school."

I was starting to understand that having someone close to you die meant hearing everyone else's saddest story.

"You lost your mother?" I said.

"Father. Listen, you probably don't want to talk about this at a party."

"Maybe not," I said, and so we talked about where she went

to school and my job at the radio station. She was studying art history at Columbia. She told me all about her roommate, Dana, whom Jonas had slept with once ("zero chemistry"), and then she asked me how my father was coping.

Sort of as an experiment, or because I had a buzz on, I decided to tell her the abridged saga of my winter, about the perfumed notes and late-night calls, how I felt sometimes like a dormitory R.A., how I'd bump into T-shirted women in the kitchen half asleep, how one of them made elaborate snacks in the middle of the night, and how another, the boutique owner, accidentally walked naked into my room, thinking it was my father's.

"Oh, please. You think she went in there by accident?" Sylvie said.

"I guess I did."

"Sweetheart. When my father died, my mother kept me away from the men she was dating." We were side by side and our arms brushed. My body tensed. "I was sixteen, and I think she thought I'd try to seduce them. And I probably would have in my own insecure way. Not literally, but enough to ruin things for her. In any event, she stayed over at their apartments. At first it was only on the weekends, but then it was like four nights a week. She'd phone to tell me to order a pizza for me and my brother, or Chinese food, whatever we wanted, and to charge it to her American Express card."

She poured me another margarita, then poured herself one. "I could have stayed out in clubs all night, or had huge-ass parties, and she would have never known. I tried it once, throwing a party, but I ended up getting too nervous about all the people there getting drunk and throwing up, so I kicked them all out."

"Did she remarry?"

"Yes, to my stepfather."

"Do you like him?"

"Better than her."

"Seriously?"

"Let's just say he's a lot less complicated."

"I find everything about my father's dating depressing."

"Depressing is when he dates a twenty-year-old."

"He hasn't done that yet."

"Then count your blessings."

I watched her after that. She was unabashed in a way that usually put me off, but in her there was something heartfelt that I latched onto. She disappeared for a half hour or so and then reappeared at my side.

"Feel like getting out of here?" she said.

"You mean the two of us?"

"You think you could do better?" she said.

I tilted my head in mock judgment. She was kind of gawky, I thought, with narrow hips and long skinny arms and an illegible word written on the back of her wrist. Her hair held the shape of a wool cap she must have worn to the party, but she didn't seem to care.

"All right. Let's go," I said.

It was Sylvie's idea to stop by our house. She wanted to meet my father "in the flesh" and see if he was as dashing as she imagined. When we reached home, Linda was camped in the kitchen, making a pot of coffee.

"Your dad went down to tell the doorman to turn up the heat," she said. She wore a cashmere V-neck sweater of my father's over a white camisole and looked like a late-career Jane Fonda. "It's freezing in here, don't you think?"

"I'm Sylvie," Sylvie said. She took off her ski cap and shook out her hair, sprinkling melting snow into the room and onto her glasses, which she removed and placed in her coat pocket.

"And I'm Linda, Andrew's dad's girlfriend," Linda said. She pulled out three mugs, one that I hadn't seen before, with the Statue of Liberty drinking coffee. She poured us cups and told us about her evening, coaching a room of Bensonhurst kids about writing résumés.

My father buzzed the intercom from downstairs and said he'd be up in ten minutes.

"When he wants things done, he goes out and gets them done," Linda said, smiling.

I could have told her that was inaccurate, that when my father wanted things done he convinced others to do them for him, but I figured she'd learn that soon enough.

"It's supposed to get down to single digits by the morning," Linda said. "Are you two in for the night?"

I pretended not to grasp what she was suggesting, but Sylvie said, "No. We just came by to warm up."

When my father came in and saw that I was with a young woman, he grinned widely. "Welcome to spring," he said. He asked Sylvie a series of questions about herself, listened with interest to her answers, and then showed her the view. There was something both wistful and very tender in the way he treated us.

We walked uptown along the park. I didn't know where we were headed, only that Sylvie appeared to have a plan.

We sat on a bench on the path at Eighty-First Street and sipped from a pint bottle of Knob Creek we'd bought at the corner liquor store, assessing the few passersby who'd braved the weather. A young guy, two or three years older than me, hobbled across on crutches.

"He's faking," Sylvie said. "Grab one of his crutches."

"What would I do with just one?"

"You could sell it back to him," she said. "Or you could beat him with it."

We traveled then to the benches near the Bandshell, where Sylvie said she used to roller-skate. I used to ride my skateboard over to watch people like her, I said.

"I was the one in the hot pants."

"Really. I think I kissed you once."

We were at the center of Central Park in the middle of the night. I thought, *This is what unbalanced people do.* Snow dropped down on us. My feet felt cold and wet, and I took another slug of whiskey. I was getting drunk. She rested her legs over mine, and I warmed them with my hands. It all felt forced, and then it didn't.

As though she'd been working up to the question, she asked me, "What's the weirdest thing you can do with your body?"

"I don't understand."

"I mean, can you do this?"

She touched her elbows together behind her head. "Or this?" She bent her hand back so that her fingertips touched the back of her forearm.

"No," I said. "Nor would I want to."

She looked so distraught that I went ahead and wiggled my left ear, something I hadn't done since grade school.

"I knew there was greatness in you," she said.

At some point, because it was on my mind, I told her about walking in the park with my mother, a week after we'd found out she was sick. I'd been away for the summer and I'd flown back to the city the day before. My mother was critiquing my wardrobe, the holes in my T-shirts and jeans.

"I'm buying you some pants," she said. "Don't be embarrassed."

"I won't," I said.

We went to some stores on Columbus Avenue, and I felt like I was eleven.

She bought me four pairs of pants, two pairs of dress socks, three shirts, and a navy peacoat. It was as though she were outfitting me for a trip. It was the first time I understood there were a finite number of afternoons we'd have together. A hundred. Ninety-nine. The next day it would be ninety-eight.

We never talked about the fact that she was dying, or what she was heading into. I think we both believed there'd be time. But it all went so quickly. The night I came to her with all the questions and thoughts I'd been saving up, her painkillers had made her so dopey she thought I was taking her to the opera. I actually played *Carmen* for her, and she said, head pressed into her pillow, that it was unbearably beautiful. She knew that she was sick, and in bed, but she thought she was young and in bed with the flu. And she asked me on one of her last days if I could make sure her tennis racket was strung, because she'd broken a string the summer before. I took it into a shop, and when they'd finished, I brought it back to show her.

When I reached her, the nurse had upped her morphine, and from then on she was gone.

When my story ended, Sylvie closed her eyes. "You know, I said everything I wanted to say to my father, and he made his peace with me. But I never played opera for him while he was in bed," she said. "That is such a fucking cool thing to do."

Outside her building Sylvie declared, "It's been a while since I slept with anyone."

I just smiled stupidly.

"You're quite adorable," she said.

Her roommate was away for the weekend. It was a pretty standard grad school apartment, two tiny bedrooms, a kitchenette, a narrow hallway, and a sunken living room decorated with a nice plush armchair and couch that must have come from someone's family. We passed out in our clothes for an hour or two. Then we slept together with them off. Undressed she was far sexier than her boyish clothes and awkward eagerness had forecast, and when she pulled me inside her, I felt irrationally as though I might have fallen in love. At around 4:00 A.M. I woke up sweating and startled from a nightmare. My mother wasn't in this one. My father had died and I was sorting through his papers and clothes, and I was showing our apartment to a series of Realtors. I asked them each, Have you seen the view over Central Park? It took some effort to determine that my father was snoring in his bed a dozen blocks away, and my relief at this understanding was so overwhelming I wept uncontrollably. In the morning I was curious to find myself in a strange apartment and not in my childhood room. I heard car horns and voices outside, a doorman's whistle. I felt tired still, but in a different way, as though I'd been drugged. I noticed then what wasn't there. The buzzing. I stumbled over to the clock on her desk—9:34.

"You can go if you want," she said from the bed.

"What do you mean?"

"I mean, I sort of trapped you here last night."

There was something fragile in her eyes I hadn't yet seen.

"I'd much rather stay," I said.

She smiled and curled into her pillow. Her feet dangled from beneath the covers.

I slipped back into bed and drew her to me so that her warm back rested against my chest. I closed my eyes, and in seconds I was out. I slept as I hadn't in years, through that whole snowy day, and when I awoke again, it was night. I threw on my pants and padded down the hallway, where I came across her reading a book on the living room sofa, legs curled beneath her. She glanced up at me. "It stopped snowing," she said. "Shall we go get a bite?"

"Yes," I said.

I grabbed the rest of my clothes from the bedroom. We bundled up and headed into the freezing night. On Broadway I felt the wind rip through my peacoat, all the way to my skin, and I was aware then that I had left the first stage of my life and was out in the world in a way I was never before.

Acknowledgments

There a lot of people I want to thank for their help during the writing of this book. The editors who published these stories and offered their sage advice: Jordan Bass, Hannah Tinti, Carol Edgarian, Dave Eggers, Kaui Hemming, Ed Schwarzchild, Evelyn Somers, and Michael Nye. My mentors and fellow writers inspired me and kept me on course: Tobias Wolff, Doug Unger, John L'Heureux, Nancy Packer, Frank Conroy, James McPherson, and Marilynne Robinson. I also want to thank Dan Chaon, Justin Cronin, and Jim Sullivan for their long and ever inspiring friendship. Jason Roberts, Ryan Harty, Eric Puchner, Peter Orner, Keith Scribner, Akhil Sharma, and Ray Isle have been trusted members of the inner circle. Great thanks to Anika Streitfeld, Laura Fraser, Elizabeth Bernstein, and Po Bronson for their close reads and their fellowship. David Berman, John Swomley, and Mark Weiner read countless drafts and offered brotherly love and advice. With great appreciation I want to thank the National Endowment for the Arts, the great women and men at the MacDowell Colony and Yaddo, the San Francisco Writers' Grotto, and my colleagues and inspiring students at California College of the Arts. David Dodson, Sandra Murray, and Shaye Hester lent me beautiful and quiet places to work. Lisa Barbash, Joy Gould Boyum, and Carol Lamberg gave their love and belief. The tireless and generous Ellen Levine was there from the start. I also want to thank the brilliant and warm-spirited folks at Ecco, especially Dan Halpern, Karen Maine, Michael McKenzie, and the remarkable Lee Boudreaux. Thanks to my parents, Joe and Heather Barbash, and to Hilary, for all and everything.